TWO MASKS ONE HEART 2
FOREVER A CLARK

A Novel

JACOB SPEARS

TRAYVON JACKSON

Good 2 Go Publishing

TWO MASKS ONE HEART 2
Written by Jacob Spears and Trayvon Jackson
Cover design: Davida Baldwin
Typesetter: Mychea
ISBN: 9781943686513

Copyright ©2016 Good2Go Publishing
Published 2016 by Good2Go Publishing
7311 W. Glass Lane • Laveen, AZ 85339
www.good2gopublishing.com
https://twitter.com/good2gobooks
G2G@good2gopublishing.com
www.facebook.com/good2gopublishing
www.instagram.com/good2gopublishing

Dedications

We would like to dedicate this book to everyone who's striving to become what's in their hearts to be. To the incarcerated women and men . . . there are no limits when living life like it's your death calling tomorrow. Stay prayed up and do your best. Free Prince Guru (Tisdale E.).

~ Jacob Spears and Trayvon Jackson

Acknowledgments

To Emma Leon Hopkins, I would like to thank you for showing me how to be a man. And my beloved sisters, Tabatha and Jennifer Hopkins, thanks for y'all's compassionate support. And last but not least in thought, I'd like to give a shout out to Clifford Wallach.

~ Jacob Spears

I'd like to thank God for letting the pen collaborate again and making me and my partner creative and talented writers. I would like to thank Good2Go Publishing for working diligently as a team and making this possible. I would like to shout out my hometown of Fort Pierce City in Martin County, Florida—y'all definitely are my #1 fans. And to my family, I love y'all. And to the one who knows these numbers best—1, 4, 3, 4, and 4—keep your head up.

~ Trayvon Jackson

Together we would like to give a shout out to Sergeant Joseph. It's people like you who make a difference in one's life.

To our fans, introduce this slide to friends and family. Be sure to tell them to do the same. For without our fans, this couldn't be called: Two Masks, One Heart II.

~ Jacob Spears and Trayvon Jackson

TWO MASKS ONE HEART 2
FOREVER A CLARK

Prelude

"I'm sick of this place," Earl said to Charles.

"Me too," Charles agreed from behind Earl while surveying the ruined buildings as they walked patrolling the lethal and filthy streets of Ramadi, Iraq.

They were in a single-file line of twelve army infantry soldiers, all awaiting a sudden attack or explosion from a mine.

"I miss home!" Earl said to Charles.

"Don't we all?" a white boy in front of Earl, named Jacob, said.

Earl had managed to escape death more than he could remember. He was now up to his neck in the tolerance of constantly being drilled and almost killed. Yesterday was the worst he'd ever seen, after having to kill a little Iraqi girl who he'd mistaken to be carrying an IED.

After taking down thirteen rebellious Taliban men, they had to battle a couple ISIL men five miles down the dirt road, where Earl was ambushed, against all odds, when trying to cut the ISIL men down from a West Wing attack. Fortunate for him, he miraculously prevailed, with the help of his friend, Charles. In months on the battlefield, Earl had transformed into a completely different man—one who his Uncle Benjamin forgot to tell him he would become.

He was addicted to killing now and was slowly advancing into a mild psychopath, only caring for one individual: Charles.

"We will rest ladies. Two hours left on this trail, and we'll come out the east to set up our watch," Sergeant Moore said to his twelve soldiers.

"Thank God! My feet are killing me!" Charles exclaimed as he sat down, placed his back against an abandoned building, and pulled out his canteen to take a swig of fresh water. Earl sat opposite Charles, out of instinct, to watch Charles's back and for Charles to watch his.

"How many more do you think you have in you, Earl?" Charles asked.

"Four . . . and it's history!" Earl retorted while using a filthy rag to wipe off the dust and sand from his M-16 rifle.

"I think I'm done after four as well," Charles said.

Boc! Boc! Boc! Boc! Boc!

The shots three miles away could be heard, but neither men could distinguish whether it was enemy fire or some random Iraqi shooting targets, such as bottles or bull's-eye targets. Everyone was tense and awaiting an attack from the Iraqis at any moment.

"What would you be doing right now if you were home?" Charles asked Earl, breaking his thoughts as he continued to clean his weapon.

"I'd probably be knee deep in some pussy. What about you?" Earl asked the same question.

"Shit, I'd be out by the river with my cousins and brothers, having a nice time . . . a barbecue and some beers."

"Sounds like fun!" Earl said.

"Hell, anywhere is fun besides here!" Jacob said, chewing on a hard piece of bread from his MRE package and washing it down with some water from his canteen.

"Amen to that, buddy!" Earl added.

"Alright, ladies. Two minutes, and break is over!" Sergeant Moore announced.

"I got a friend named Jake, the first white boy that I've ever seen who could barbecue like no other, and he has his own special sauce that he uses," Charles said.

"Man, I miss real food," Earl retorted as he stood up.

"Okay, ladies. Let's move it!" the sergeant commanded everyone.

Earl and Charles were once again in line, one behind the other, walking on the dirt road in the hot environment.

"So, Jacob, how soon until you're trying to get back to Kentucky?" Earl asked the young man marching in front of him.

"Soon as I finish four . . . and not in a box!" Jacob answered.

The twelve men walked for two hours on the narrow dirt road, until they came to an abandoned temple in Ramadi. They passed burnt cars, schools, and churches that were all destroyed by ISIL when they took the city from the Iraqis.

Damn, this shit looks crazy for real, Earl thought to himself as the rest of his fellow soldiers walked inside the ruined temple to inspect for danger.

"We will camp here and resume on the first sight of day," the sergeant ordered. "Come . . . and let's inspect the buildings surrounding us!"

When the men stepped out of the temple and made it to the middle of the street, a deadly fusillade erupted from the abandoned buildings, dropping the off-guard men one by one.

Boom! Boom!

Tat! Tat! Tat! Tat!

Chop! Chop! Chop!

"Incoming fire!" Sergeant Moore screamed, returning fire with his men.

Bop! Bop! Bop! Bop!

Chop! Chop!

Earl backed himself to the wall and squatted while returning fire.

Now or never, Earl thought as he trained his weapon on Sergeant Moore and fired, making his head explode in a spray of blood and brain matter. He had wanted Sergeant Moore for the longest time and now had him.

"Who's the lady now?" Earl questioned, resuming fighting off the enemy.

Charles, when trying to cross to the other side of the road, was cut down by two slugs entering his thighs and leg.

"Awww, shit!" Charles cried out, simultaneously dragging his legs and making an effort to still cross.

"Shit!" Earl yelled, running toward Charles and swiftly grabbing ahold of the back of his vest. He then began dragging him across the road while Charles returned fire.

Earl had made it to the back of a burning car when two slugs entered his stomach and right shoulder, dropping him to his knees.

I'm about to die, he thought as another slug entered his side, taking his face to the dirt. All Earl could ever remember was Charles dragging him by his vest to the other side of the burning car, where they would be safe until death came to take them away.

1

Staring outside her parents' bedroom window, she watched the squirrels chase after each other on the ancient oak tree. The sight was intriguing, as was the sun, which had been revived after the stormy days. Her thoughts were on her parents and the sudden disaster that had come into her life. Despite the joy that nature gives me from its beautiful sight, I am still hurt, where my soul seems unforgiving, she reflected.

A noise from behind startled Shaquana out of her thoughts. When she turned around, she saw Maurice walking through the door, followed by his heavy scent of Polo cologne.

"Sorry, baby, if I frightened you," he said as he continued into the opulent bedroom. He wrapped his arms around her and held her from behind.

"It's okay. I was just thinking of something."

She's always thinking, he thought while kissing her on the nape of her neck.

"What are you thinking about?" Maurice asked her, already knowing where her train of thought had been lately.

She talked about her mother and father daily and cried herself to sleep almost every night. Since their funerals, Shaquana had built a shell around herself, only allowing Maurice into her world. She had quit school immediately to avoid the dry and feigned condolences from her classmates and to avoid explaining her breakup with her best friend, who had betrayed her by sleeping with her father.

"I was thinking of dad's last words to me," Shaquana started while still watching the squirrels chase each other.

At first it had been two squirrels. Now there were two chasing one squirrel with a nut. When Shaquana was in one of these moments, Maurice had quickly learned to just listen to her vent. She got no reply. But beyond a dubious thought, she knew that she had his undivided attention. He was her champion and lover who showed her more than enough compassion.

He cares, Shaquana considered before saying, "He told me when I was worried . . ." She paused, fighting to hold back a storm of tears. ". . . that without him, I was to do what a Clark would do . . ." Unfortunately, I have no clue what duties a Clark does, she wanted to say. But the silence and warm comfort from Maurice's consoling assuaged her.

She continued to watch the squirrels now chase the falling nut to the ground, as the one squirrel that possessed it initially had dropped it. I guess that's life in all aspects, she thought of the squirrel losing the nut. "What is lost becomes someone else's treasure. I wonder whose treasure Mom and Dad became?" she broke the silence. "Maurice, what did he do? Why did my mom die, too?" Shaquana broke down, questioning Maurice, who only had part of the truth. But he would not let her hear it from him or anyone else. He held her like always and let her cry in his arms.

"It's not your fault, boo!" Maurice said, turning her around and embracing her tightly.

Shaquana's body shook violently as she cried hysterically.

Damn! Why she let herself get to this point every time, Maurice thought. All the crying in the world can't bring no one back from the grave.

Since her parents' deaths and funerals, Shaquana buried herself in her parents' bedroom and made it hers, turning her room into a guest room. She rarely was seen out of the house, or downstairs, where Brenda and Maurice would talk every morning over coffee and breakfast. Jerome, Brenda's boyfriend, would join them as well. They all were constantly praying that Shaquana's would abate her grief, break out of her depression shell, and see life from their perspective: that everyone was subject to death. And it made no difference of how it came, because it was all inevitable.

Maurice picked up Shaquana and carried her over to their king-sized bed. He lay her on her back and then slowly removed her silk robe that had belonged to her mother. Underneath she was nude and growing thin in areas she'd once been curvy, such as her hips and lower body. As she continued to cry, Maurice kissed her body passionately, from her breasts to her sultry mound between her legs.

"Baby, it's okay," he whispered.

"Maurice!" she moaned out, rubbing the back of his head as he made love to her with his tongue, converting her cries to moans of pleasure.

She loved Maurice and appreciated him for his support and showing her that she was important to him. What the streets had going on was irrelevant, and Maurice reminded her every night and time, like now, that he was there for her.

3

"Make love to me, Maurice," she demanded, gyrating her hips simultaneously as Maurice's tongued titillated her throbbing clitoris.

"I will baby. I'm here," Maurice retorted.

"Shit!" she moaned out in pleasure.

He was everything to her, and their love was genuine, no doubt. But despite the bliss and sweet comfort, it was like an Advil subsiding a severe headache: the pain would always return.

* * *

Lying in bed unable to move or scream, she watched the dark figure continue to walk slowly through the door, making his way to her side of the bed. Beside her was her lover, and it was evident that he was asleep or . . . Oh my God! Is he okay? Tameka thought, once again having failed attempts at screaming. Help me! the words in her mind could find no voice. When trying to open her mouth, her jaw bone seemed like it weighed a ton, not allowing her to operate her body parts with her own will.

The dark figure came closer. Despite the darkness in the room, she was able to see its every move clearly.

I can't believe this. Jarvis, please wake up! she thought, hoping that her thoughts could be heard in some type of telepathic way. But there was no telepathic connection between her and Jarvis.

The figure came closer, passing the moon illuminating through the beach house window, and Tameka caught a glimpse of the figure. His face structure was one of a kind. She took notice almost immediately.

4

It can't be! she thought, with the beat of her heart increasing to the point of it feeling as if it was about to explode in her chest.

The figure now stood over her, and she had no control to flee or voice to scream. A light from a lighter in the figure's hand flickered and illuminated the room. When she looked at the figure, a face that she knew well stared back at her.

Benjamin! How? You are dead! she thought before she began to scream hysterically, finally hearing herself. Tameka unconsciously leapt up from the bed, where she saw blood imbued everywhere, soaked into the bed, and Jarvis's throat cut from ear to ear.

"Noooo!" she screamed out in rage until she woke up out of her slumber, sweating excessively.

She looked over at Jarvis and found him sleeping peacefully, and the figure that turned out to be Benjamin was gone.

Damn! This man is haunting me! she thought, wiping the sweat from her face with her hands. She took notice that her body was trembling as she emerged from bed and walked to the bathroom, where she stood at the luxurious sink and splashed cold water on her face.

She and Jarvis were still in Mexico renting a beach house in Cancun. Despite the new lavish lifestyle and love, Tameka found more sleepless nights than comfort. And she sometimes deeply wondered if she had killed the right man. She never told Jarvis of her nightmares, because she felt that they were personal, and no man could fix this type of situation.

What the hell can Jarvis or anyone else do to a dead man? she wanted to know.

She looked in the mirror at herself and imagined that Benjamin was behind her. She was naked and cupped her breast in her hand while fondling her erect nipples. Tameka closed her eyes and hated herself for letting money keep her from a good man. But she had no choice. It was either Jarvis or die with Benjamin. He's going to haunt me until he's satisfied, Tameka realized.

"If a dead man could speak for his vengeance, what would he want done?" Tameka asked herself.

Return, Benjamin, and tell me what it is that you want, Tameka thought, already knowing the answer if a dead man could talk. She just didn't have the stomach to do it, despite the many times she'd thought about it.

"No, I can't!" she whispered to herself.

2

"Clark, get dressed. You have a visit," the female deputy called out over the intercom in his cell.

I wonder who it is? Daquan wondered.

It had been almost six months since his parents' death, something that had changed him completely and given him an I-don't-give-a-fuck attitude.

Unlike at the juvenile facility, where they wore yellow jumpsuits, the inmates in Jonesboro County Jail wore orange. The level of their felonies was recognized by distinctive wristbands of various colors. Daquan's wristband was yellow, which represented capital murder. In his cell block, there were only a few cats sporting the yellow wristband with Daquan. He strapped on his black Bob Barker shoes and then walked out of his cell and cell block altogether, to the visitation room adjacent to the cell block's hallway.

When he came through the chatty atmosphere, he saw that it was a full house. As he passed inmates conversing with their families behind the bulletproof glass, he was hit with a wave of emotion when he thought of the last person who'd been to see him. It was Renae's visit in his head and her face he saw as he sat down at his booth. But he knew that it was only the reflection of her . . . and that person sitting there was only his Auntie Brenda.

Damn, she looks too much like Mom, he thought as he lifted the phone to his ear. On Brenda's face was a compassionate smile in an effort to cheer up her nephew.

"Hey, baby. How are you?" Brenda asked Daquan while waving at him.

He could tell that she was trying her best to keep from breaking down. The last he'd seen her was at his parents' funeral, where she passed out, and woke up in a hospital bed.

"I'm getting by, Auntie. How are you?" he asked.

Brenda blinked her eyes two times as tears came in a flood with a broken voice full of grief, pain, and stress.

"Daquan, it's hard. Shaquana is not speaking with me, and we might be losing Grandma. It's burdensome. I'd been contemplating on coming months ago, Daquan, but I'm too weak . . . without my sister," Brenda broke down crying hysterically.

Damn! I thought I was taking it bad. My aunt is experiencing something far deeper than the loss of a sister, compared to a son's grief of losing his mom and dad, Daquan thought. He was holding his head up for his Auntie, despite the pain that he was hiding on the inside.

"Auntie Brenda, things will look up for us. But we can't let what's out of our control tear us down," Daquan said to his aunt.

Stay strong, nigga. Don't break! Daquan introspectively told himself.

"You're right, Daquan. We will get through this," Brenda exclaimed, simultaneously wiping her eyes with a napkin.

"How's Earl?" Daquan asked, wondering why he hadn't seen his cousin at the funeral.

Brenda shook her head from side to side, on the verge of breaking down again. With that gesture, Daquan quickly assumed the worst.

"Please don't tell me Earl's dead, Auntie!"

"Daquan . . . ," she said, pausing to wipe her eyes again. It was a score for her that she didn't wear makeup, or else it would be smeared everywhere on her face, which was identical to his mom's.

"Earl was shot, Daq—"

"Nooo, Auntie. No!"

"Daquan, he's okay. Don't worry!" Brenda quickly responded to her nephew, who'd almost lost control and broken down himself.

"What's wrong? Where is he?" Daquan asked.

"He's at a rehabilitation facility. He . . . lost his right leg," Brenda exclaimed, battling the surge of emotion.

"His leg?" Daquan retorted.

"He has a metal leg now, like a robot," Brenda said smiling, once she'd remembered how Earl was taking the loss of his leg better than her. "Earl says it's just a leg."

"Just a leg!" Daquan exclaimed frivolously, with a hint of a grin.

"Yes, boy! He had the nerve to say it's just a damn leg!" Brenda responded.

"Maybe it's more meaning to him. You know . . . something like a souvenir," Daquan said.

"Who knows what Earl is thinking! He received a purple heart because it was in the line of duty— something like that. You know I don't understand that mess."

"Me either," Daquan retorted.

"So, Daquan, when was the last time you spoke with your lawyer?"

"Do I still have a lawyer? I haven't seen him since he last came and saw me when they brought me over here."

"Really?" Brenda answered.

"Serious!" Daquan exclaimed.

"I will call him after I leave here to see what the problem is, Daquan . . ."

"Please do, Auntie. Because he don't return none of my calls, and it's a lot of frustration," he informed her.

"I promise you I will do that for you. Meantime, Daquan, I need you to stay out of trouble . . . and stay in your prayers and Bible . . ."

Bible! Ain't no God in me! Daquan thought, but instead of letting his Auntie hear his true feelings about his faith, he responded, "Yes, ma'am." Changing the subject, he then asked, "Auntie Brenda, how bad is Grandma?"

"Daquan, grandma lost both of her legs from her diabetes illness and is constantly going into stroke after stroke."

Damn! Why do I feel like my family has been cursed? Daquan asked himself, judging from all the tribulations in his life so suddenly.

"All we can do is pray for her, Daquan."

If praying won't bring back my mom and dad, then it sure ain't about to save my dour grandmother, Daquan thought.

"Is Shaquana getting my letters?" Daquan asked curiously, already knowing that she was receiving all of his mail.

"All of your letters to Shaquana go under her door, or Maurice takes them to her"

"Maurice? Who is that?" Daquan asked, perplexed from not recalling the name.

10

"Maurice is your sister's new boyfriend who—"

"She can lay up with fucking strangers, but not write, come see, or pick up the phone for her little brother, and y'all just let her be on that flaw-ass shit!" Daquan yelled out in a surging rage of hurt and betrayal.

"Daquan, lis—"

"No, Auntie Brenda. Nobody listens to how Daquan feels. My mom is dead and my dad. That means I have nobody but me. I should have seen this shit, but I just didn't want to believe it!" Daquan said with tears falling from his eyes.

With nothing else to say, Daquan hung up the phone on his Auntie and walked away from the booth—and the visitation room altogether—never looking back.

3

On the other side of the Jonesboro County Jail, in the west wing, Tittyboo sat in his cell, on his bottom bunk, reading an erotic fiction book by Zane. Since his arrival, he'd put on ten extra pounds to his already stubby frame. Eating, sleeping, and reading were all that he did throughout the day. His canteen was a consistent flow, coming from Shay, who had worked out a deal with the DA's office to testify against Tittyboo and Daquan—unbeknownst to either of them.

Damn, I'm hungry, he thought while rubbing his enormous stomach.

He marked his book on page 41 and then laid it on the bunk.

That nigga Bruce is a maniac! Tittyboo thought while opening up his locker underneath his bunk.

He was loaded with a variety of junk food and ramen noodle soups.

"I think I'll make another goulash," Tittyboo mumbled to himself while digging through the locker.

"Yo, Titty. What you about to cook?" Tittyboo's friend Joshah asked as he walked through the doorway of the cell.

Joshah was twenty-three years old and was looking at a long bid after being caught up in a rape case against an eighteen-year-old white woman who worked at a hotel in Jonesboro. Like 90 percent of all inmates, he proclaimed that he was innocent. He was originally from East Atlanta, had a caramel complexion, and was five nine and 148 pounds. He was a goofy-looking cat with protruding bunny teeth. He was straight with Tittyboo because he knew how to gamble, cheat, and win.

"Yeah, I'm about to start in a minute," Tittyboo exclaimed as he tossed six chicken ramen noodles and two packs of tuna onto his bunk.

"Oh, shit! Titty's about to throw down in this motherfucker!" Tittyboo's cellmate, Lamar, exclaimed as he walked in the cell sweaty from working out in the dorm's dayroom.

Lamar was a tall oil-black-ass nigga from Bankhead, who got caught in a club shooting two years ago that killed two College Park girls. All of his codefendants pointed fingers at him, and the weapon—like Tittyboo's—had his prints on it.

Lamar grabbed his towel and washcloth off the hook attached to the wall, and his shower slides from under Tittyboo's bunk on the floor

"How much do I have to put in?" Lamar asked, wanting to participate in the goulash by contributing to the necessities.

Despite his consideration, Tittyboo was straight with his cellmate, and Lamar knew Tittyboo's heart: If he had it, then Lamar was always welcome to it.

"Nigga, why you always asking that dumb question? You know you already in on this shit automatically, nigga!" Tittyboo said, pointing his index finger at Lamar in a frolicsome manner.

"Damn! My nigga! I be just wanting to pitch in sometimes," Lamar exclaimed.

"You cool, shawty. Trust that!" Tittyboo replied.

"Ten-four, fat boy," Lamar said as he walked out of the cell toward the shower area.

"Now, do you have any stupid-ass questions too? When you know that your ass is in too," Tittyboo said to Joshah, who sat on his chrome toilet.

"Naw. I was going to ask—"

"Shit!" Tittyboo retorted, cutting off Joshah mid-sentence.

*   *   *

Since Benjamin's death, Champagne had been battling depression. Without Benjamin, her world was crushed. Then the miscarriage only made matters worse for her. Deep down she felt like shit, because not only had she lost the man she loved and their child, but she also had lost a real friend . . . one that was close to her like a sister.

My stupid treachery! she realized while lying in her bed, the only place that held comfort for her.

She'd been awake and heard her grandmother humming an old-school hit that she was way too young to understand or know. She hated lying to her grandmother about her fallout with Shaquana.

How can she continue to hold that shit against me? Whatever happened to forgiveness? Champagne wanted to know.

She sat up in bed and grabbed her iPhone that was lying on the nightstand beside her.

"I guess I'll see if she's okay," she said after a long sigh.

Champagne logged onto her Facebook page and entered a note into Shaquana's inbox: Friends are supposed to forgive, Shaquana. As a woman, I'm sorry, and I love you. Please . . . let's talk.

Champagne sighed before she sent the brief message to Shaquana.

14

Shit is just not the same without Shaquana, Champagne had to admit. Without Benjamin or Chad, she was just like the hoodlums who were sucking dick and selling their bodies for money. Although she hadn't gotten to that point, she knew that it would be inevitable if she didn't find some source of income. Both Benjamin and Chad had made sure that she had money in her pockets. She'd dropped out of high school because she didn't want to explain their breakup.

I have to find me a job, she thought, emerging from bed in her Mickey and Minnie pajamas. As she walked to her closet to find something sexy to put on, a prospect came to mind.

"I heard that Maurice is living with her. Maybe he could hook me and her back up!" Champagne said as she scrolled through her contacts on her iPhone.

"Bingo!" she retorted when she came upon Maurice's number. As she tapped his number to connect, she held her breath momentarily. When the phone rang twice, she sighed in relief, but was upset when she heard the connection fail.

"This number is no longer in service," the operator announced.

"Bitch!" she screamed in a whisper so that her grandmother wouldn't hear her frustration and outburst. "For as long as I knew this nigga, he ain't never changed his number," Champagne said while going onto Maurice's Facebook page, where she found his profile picture changed to display a picture of him and Shaquana hugged up, looking like the lovers they were.

"Okay, Mr. Love boy," Champagne said, then sent Maurice a message: Mr. Lover boy please contact me ASAP. And please don't avoid me, or else! We know the truth. Her heart can only stand so much! XO for old time's sake.

4

The conspicuous lime-green '72 Impala sat tall on its 32-inch Forgiato Turbiante custom rims. Romel's thunderous bass rattled the windows of the projects on 3rd Street in College Park—and even three blocks away. Since Chad's death, Romel had stepped in his shoes and was still competing with the niggas on 12th Street, who loyalty remained with Maurice. He was someone who Romel had been desperately waiting to run across, but he had no source to reveal the directions to where Romel could find him slipping. Romel pulled into the crowded parking lot at the neighborhood community park, where a lot of action was taking place, just like every Sunday.

"Damn, this bitch on swole today!" Romel said, unable to hear himself over his loud music. Pastor Troy emanated loud from his 6 x 9 tweeters and six 12-inch speakers in his spacious trunk.

People were turning their heads and contemplating leaving because of the troubled atmosphere and aura that followed Romel, and what people already knew: that Romel, like Chad, had a death wish upon him. With his Choppa AK-47 rifle riding shotgun with him, Romel was dying to open up a nigga scalp whenever and wherever it started. Romel paraded through the crowd, paying close attention to the sexy women who wore their best fuck-me outfits. He wasn't a man committed to a woman or any relationship, so he was free to roam and snatch any bitch he wanted. After cutting off his dreadlocks in an effort to stay low-key and avoid Maurice's wrath, Romel turned the women on more with the low-boy cut. He parked backward next to a red bitch covered in tattoos, who was also sitting on the hood of her red Lexus coupe.

"Damn, who is this bitch?" he asked.

She held a bottle of Cîroc in her hand, between her thick stallion thighs. It was peach—the state's official fruit.

She had on some army camouflage boy shorts that crawled into the crack of her curves in her pelvic area. Her matching blouse was a blow-out, revealing her bare back, with a V-cut in the front showing off her juicy red breasts. On her head, she had a matching snap-back hat with a big letter A for Atlanta.

"She gotta be from the city," Romel said as he emerged from his car, simultaneously pulling the top back to reveal the luxurious inside of his ride.

When he looked over at the redbone chick, who was beyond the word beautiful, he saw that she was all into him. Their eye contact spoke precisely of their immediate attraction for one another.

"Nice car!" she said in a sweet Janet Jackson voice.

"Thank you, shawty. The same for you, too," he replied. "So tell me. How come I never seen you around?" he asked curiously, being cautious.

Despite her beauty, Romel knew well of the flipside to a bad bitch. It could be death or a nigga being set up by the feds. And from Romel's perspective, he was subject to and due for them both.

"That's because I'm not from around here," she answered him while watching Romel admire her and her nice Lexus. Romel walked out into the road so he could get a view of the front of her car, and got a full view of her pussy print bulging through her camouflage shorts.

"Damn!" he exclaimed, thinking out loud, unable to bridle his lust. "I mean . . . damn! Your ride is hot!" Romel said immediately in an effort to cure his lustful outburst.

"It's okay. I hear it all the time. Don't act like you so all into my ride, because that's shady," the beautiful woman shot back.

"What do they call you?" Romel asked.

She looked him up and down in his Gucci outfit and Mauri boots, and saw that he was worth a try. And her opportunity had presented the perfect chance that she'd so desperately needed.

"My name is Markeina. I'm from Florida, but I was born in Bankhead . . ."

Bankhead from Florida. No wonder, he thought.

"So, what's your name?" she asked, already knowing his full government name.

"They call me Romel. So who is your people?"

"I have none. I'm solo, nigga, because a man can't do shit that money can't do for me," Markeina exclaimed.

"I like that attitude," he retorted.

"And I like your understanding," Markeina said, tilting back the Cîroc bottle for a long swig.

As she drank, Romel stared at the plumped mound bulging between her legs, and she watched him as well, unbeknownst to him.

* * *

Shaquana, baby, at least hear what she has to say."

"No, Maurice. Now please drop the subject!" she yelled out to him before she stormed off into the bathroom to take a hot shower. When the door slammed behind her, Maurice released a sigh of frustration.

Champagne had begged him in tears to make Shaquana forgive her. She'd tried forcing herself on him, to no avail because Maurice's loyalty to Shaquana stood too firm. Despite her continued betrayal acts and trying to come on to her friend's man, Maurice still had pity for her.

After making love to Shaquana, he told her a lie about seeing Champagne in the neighborhood and having a talk with her. He told Shaquana everything except for meeting Champagne at a Jamaican restaurant in Atlanta. He was still getting money out in College Park and lurking for Romel while simultaneously waiting to cross paths again with Haitian Beny.

Maurice knew that Beny wasn't about to sleep, knowing that he wasn't the one who killed Benjamin. In fact, he wasn't sure if Beny killed Benjamin himself or if another enemy wanted him and his wife dead. So he played five moves ahead of Haitian Beny—and that was being prepared. He was prepared to face him and whoever wanted Benjamin and his wife dead.

Maurice emerged from bed and walked into the bathroom, where Shaquana was in the steaming hot shower. He stared at her through the glass but was only able to see her figure, which alone revived his manhood.

I'ma give this one more try, but first I'ma fuck the shit out her. I love this bitch, and her stubbornness, he thought as he stepped into the shower and made love to the woman who'd stolen his heart.

But when the topic came up of forgiving Champagne, Shaquana was standing adamantly strong again as she shouted, "Hell nooo!"

5

"That's good, Mr. Davis," the beautiful rehabilitation therapist named Katrina remarked as she walked into Earl's room.

Earl was just finishing up a set of push-ups, and his muscular frame was dripping with sweat, completely turning on Katrina.

"Hey there!" he said, pulling himself up from the ground by grabbing hold of the support bar attached to the wall

"Good news or bad news first?" Katrina asked, tossing Earl a towel to dry the sweat from his face and body as he sat on his bed.

"Good news doesn't last long, so give me the bad news first," Earl stated.

Katrina walked up to him, a clipboard in her hand and dressed in doctor's scrubs.

"Well, the bad news is I won't be able to see you every day no more, because of your discharge from our facility."

"Really? I thought I had another month to go," Earl retorted in elation. Damn, this is a dream come true, he thought. "So, what is the good news?"

"The good news is that maybe we could have dinner sometime this week on my day off, and see where things go from there. I think it's only right for me to continue to treat you," Katrina said seductively while staring into Earl's handsome eyes.

Both of them had an irrefutable chemistry for the other, and they had admired one another on a sexual level on many occasions. There had been plenty of times that Katrina had wanted to make her move on Earl, but her career was one that she had worked hard to obtain. And there was no man worth her throwing it all away.

She was five five and had a gorgeous caramel complexion. One would think she'd be married to some big-shot lawyer or doctor, but she wasn't, which gave Earl a head start to explore her world and conclude why there was so much of a gap in her life, beautiful as she was.

"That is indeed good news beautiful," Earl said.

"Well, sign here," she said, tossing the clipboard into Earl's lap. "And date on the yellow line. Before you leave, an accountant from the facility will assist you with setting up your Social Security income."

"What about Charles? How's he coming along?" Earl asked about his friend and the man who saved his life.

"Charles told me to tell you that he is doing fine and is ready to barbecue," Katrina informed him.

"So, he's back home . . . not next door?" Earl retorted.

"He's home as of two days ago," Katrina said. "So I guess that the goods news wasn't what you were expecting, huh?" she asked him.

He seemed nonchalant about the prospect of them getting together, as he was more looking forward to meeting up with Charles. It really bothered Katrina to even think of it like that, but nothing in life seemed surprising to her.

Friends are closer than anything these days, Katrina thought.

Katrina waited on Earl to complete his paperwork and reply to her good news.

23

"You're probably wondering why I ain't answering you yet, huh?" Earl asked, passing the clipboard back to Katrina.

"Exactly!" she answered.

"Because you know exactly how I feel about dinner. And you know that once I leave this commercial site and am out of the sight of these swines' turf, I'm going to hold you in my arms like no man has ever done," Earl said, looking directly into Katrina's adorable eyes that held back water.

"Let them be tears of joy, baby, not pain," he retorted.

"Yes, sir," Katrina said, smiling bright as she then walked out of the room a happy woman who was ready to take a chance with loving a man again.

* * *

When Haitian Beny pulled up to Money Green Records studios in his black Suburban, he felt like the boss he was. With Benjamin out of the way, a lot of old venues had opened up for him. And for those who weren't up on his history, the old timers laced them quickly. The niggas in the dope game capitulated to Beny's warning of wrath, for they wanted no problems with him or his steadily growing force. To keep the envy at bay, Beny let Jarvis regulate Jonesboro, just as long as he stayed on the same team.

Jarvis was back in town, and it was time for their monthly meet. Big Funk and Corey walked into the studio with Beny and immediately heard Antron's recording. Since Jarvis took over, he signed Antron to a $20 million contract that wouldn't expire until the next decade. And instead of receiving 10 percent of his royalties, Jarvis gave him the real game and let him profit 30 percent of his royalties. He also explained to Antron how Benjamin was getting over on him big time—something that hurt Antron and made him quickly dislike the blood of a Clark.

Walking by the recording studio booth, Beny threw a peace sign to Antron, who returned the same greeting. White boy David returned the same greeting as well before Beny proceeded down the hallway en route to Benjamin's old office—now taken over by Jarvis.

When the trio arrived at the door, Beny knocked twice.

"Come in," Jarvis said.

When Beny and his two bodyguards stepped inside the opulent office that Jarvis had completely transformed, erasing the taste of Benjamin from the face of the earth, they saw him sitting at his desk.

The leather sofa was replaced with a brown suede one with bamboo. Pictures of Z-Pac and Jay-Z were on the walls in large frames, and his desk was an elegant cherry and oak wood antique model from Italy. Jarvis stood in his white Armani suit and greeted his company with a firm handshake.

"Good to see you all," Jarvis said.

"And it's good to see you back in town, Jarvis. Where is Tameka?" Beny asked.

"Oh, she's over at the club setting up things for tonight," Jarvis responded.

"So tell me. What's good?" Jarvis inquired, with his hands locked behind his head.

"Jarvis, have you seen Maurice around?" Beny asked from the sofa.

"I've been back three days, Beny, and haven't been lingering around Jonesboro. But I could . . ."

"Don't worry about looking for him. My sources are reliable. How do you feel about Benjamin's house?" Haitian Beny asked.

"I have no interest in the man's home," Jarvis replied.

"Well I do! And if Maurice is in there, like my sources tell me, then I plan on getting him to come out," Beny said with a mischievous smile on his face.

6

When Mr. Goodman walked into his plush office, his visitor was awaiting him, sitting in a comfortable chair in front of his ornate oak desk.

Damn, that smells good, Mr. Goodman thought, taking in the aroma of his visitor's perfume by Rihanna.

"Good morning, Ms. Davis. It's nice to see that you've made it on time," Mr. Goodman said, extending his hand from across the table to shake Brenda's hand.

"And it's a pleasure to meet you, Mr. Goodman. I believe the last time we saw each other was at my nephew's court date," Brenda said in a mildly stern manner.

"Well, if you would have attended his plea arraignment, I'm positive that you would have seen me again, Ms. Davis . . ."

"Call me Brenda, please," she fired back.

"Yes, I will. How can I help you on anything?" Because I'm ready to dismiss your drama ass, Mr. Goodman wanted to say, but he kept it professional.

"Obviously I'm here to talk about my nephew, Mr. Goodman," she said before she paused to observe him for a second.

"When was the last time you spoke with my nephew concerning his case, sir?" she asked.

"Well, to be frank with you, Brenda, I've stopped seeing Daquan until further notice. Months ago . . ."

Bitch! she wanted to scream out, but she remained calm.

"Mr. Benjamin Clark, before his death, only paid me $45,000 to represent Daquan as a juvenile."

"So what you're trying to tell me is you're in need of more funds to fully represent him, correct?" Brenda said with spice in her voice.

"Brenda, let me explain something to you. The policy is that I can easily remove myself from the case after ninety days of failure to pay. But being that this is Benjamin's son, I've continued to remain on the docket to prevent your nephew from falling into the hands of some sorry nonchalant public defender . . . better known as a public pretender," he said with emphasis while staring into her eyes.

After hearing how he had saved her nephew from simply becoming a statistic of a nonchalant lawyer who received the same paycheck and salary whether he or she won or lost a case, her attitude quickly left and was replaced by an appreciative spirit.

"Thank you, Mr. Goodman, for having patience. But tell me, why haven't you tried getting in touch with someone in my family?" Brenda asked.

Mr. Goodman quickly logged on to his computer, and pulled up Daquan's file in no time. He clicked his mouse twice and turned around the monitor so Brenda could view it.

"Ms. . . . I mean Brenda, I've been sending the immediate emergency contact a letter every month," Goodman said, pointing to his data and revealing the next of kin name and address to be Ms. Pearl Davis.

Wow! Momma could have at least told me . . . and Renae and Benjamin should've had me as their next of kin, she thought while looking at the screen, dumbfounded.

"Sorry, Mr. Goodman, but my mother has been ill lately and . . . I am the next of kin," Brenda informed him.

"Well then it's you who I need to be talking to," Mr. Goodman explained.

He stood and walked over to a file cabinet behind his desk. As he searched for Daquan's file, Brenda took in his elegant, slim six three frame and, for a second, thought about being coquettish, for she knew that $45,000 wasn't close to what Daquan would need for good representation.

It isn't like it isn't in me. Shit! Good as my pussy is, it'll make a saint turn cloak, she thought of her prospect of seducing Mr. Goodman.

"There we go!" Mr. Goodman said after a long sigh.

He returned to his seat and opened up a file containing Daquan's case information.

"Okay, Brenda. First-degree murder with a firearm. Cindy Mendor and Migerle Pierre. Two counts. If he's found guilty, it will land him on death row."

"Who's his prosecutor?" Brenda inquired.

"I won't know until I get back on his case . . ."

"So, we going to go there?" Brenda retorted in her sexy voice.

Bitch! Don't try it, Mr. Goodman thought, catching on to Brenda's sorry-ass attempts. I know the art of seduction well.

"Frankly, yes. But for Benjamin, I will cut back on the price and give you a big break"

"And what is a big break?" Brenda asked. "Is you crazy—$140,000?" Brenda screamed while jumping up from her seat. "That is not no cutback, Mr. Goodman! I'm not Benjamin, and he sure ain't leave no money laying around for his kids. He cared too much for his homeboys instead. All I have is the house, Mr. Goodman, and a little cash in my account, but not what you're asking for!" she exclaimed in such a conniption that she was unconsciously tearing up.

Before she knew it, Mr. Goodman had hastened over to her in two longs strides and was holding her in his long, slender arms. The smell of his Jordan cologne and his warming embrace made her think of Jerome.

Would he help me? she thought.

"It's okay, Brenda. How much is the house worth?" Mr. Goodman asked.

He can't be serious, she thought, shaking her head from side to side, unable to stop the tears from falling from the wells of her eyes.

"I can't give you their house. That's all they have," she said, pulling away from him.

"Brenda, if Daquan wins, I'll let them pay the house out of the mortgage."

"And what if he lose?" she retorted.

"Then it'll be up to you to pay for the house out of the mortgage," he said.

"Let me think about this," Brenda said, wiping her eyes with a tissue she'd taken off of Mr. Goodman's desk.

"I'll be expecting your call or visit. Thank you for stopping by," he said, helping Brenda to the door.

"Okay," she said as she left this office.

As she drove away from the high-rise law firm in her black BMW, her mind went back to Daquan's frustrations.

Shit would operate a lot better if Shaquana could get her head in the game. Here it is, your brother is looking at death row, and you're too busy worrying about . . . two lost souls, Brenda thought as she got on the interstate and returned back to Jonesboro. I'm going to pull that heifer out of that room my damn self, Brenda thought as her iPhone began ringing. When she saw who the caller was, her face lit up with joy.

"Hey, baby, please tell me you're in town," Brenda said.

"I'm at the house, and your son is refusing to let me inside, and he even pulled out his toy on me," Jerome screamed into the phone.

"Toy!" Brenda retorted.

"Yeah, toy . . . as in gun, Brenda!"

"Baby, I'm on my way. Where is he at?" Brenda asked, confused. From her understanding, she wasn't expecting Earl to come home until next month.

"He's inside!" Jerome said with emphasis. "And I'm locked outside."

"Baby, I'm a block away. I'm coming," she said, disconnecting the call while simultaneously accelerating to her home.

When she pulled into her driveway next to Jerome's silver Chevy Tahoe, she saw that he was frustrated. As she got out of the truck, she ran up to him and embraced him.

"I'm so sorry, baby. I had no clue that he would be home so soon," Brenda admitted.

"It's okay. It's time to put an end to this shit today," Jerome said.

He wasn't a coward, and had every means to prove that to his stepson, for the love he had for Brenda went beyond measure.

"Let's go!" Brenda said, walking toward her front door with her arms wrapped around Jerome's waist.

She put her key into the door, and she and Jerome walked into her luxurious home that Benjamin had bought for her years ago.

"Earl, where are you?" she screamed into the house for her son while Jerome walked into the living room and sat down on the black leather sofa. He observed the many pictures of him and Brenda, and saw that most of them had his face marked out with a black permanent marker.

Son of a bitch! Jerome thought.

He heard Earl descend the stairs, and stood up. When their eyes met, both of them held fire in them and—like lions—they clashed.

"Earl, stop it!" Brenda screamed as both men went blow for blow in her living room. Both men were strong and reputable fighters.

Stunned at what she was seeing, Brenda fell to her knees crying. "Lord, help me! Please Lord!" she cried out.

"Arrgghh!" Earl groaned out as he lifted Jerome and slammed him onto the glass table in the middle of the living room.

Smash!

Immediately, he got on top of Jerome and punched him repeatedly in his face. Jerome was dazed from the blows, so he covered his face by grabbing ahold of Earl's arms. Earl was unable to pound Jerome like he wanted to, so he began head-butting Jerome, who then let go of Earl, for the impact was severe and had him semiconscious. When Earl went to pound Jerome by cocking his arm back, Brenda dove onto Jerome's body, a move that halted Earl's plans.

"Stop it, Earl! Please! Stop it!" she screamed at the top of her lungs.

"How could you, Mom? This ain't no man . . . !"

"Then what makes you one!" she screamed back at her son, who became speechless.

"Leave now! I mean it. Leave!" Brenda screamed, with tears cascading down her face. Earl's face was covered in blood, and at the moment, she did not know the creature that stared back at her.

"I have no problem leaving," Earl said.

7

Pop that pussy, bitch, and work them walls for daddy, the lyrics of Antron's hit serenaded from the subwoofers at Pleasers, along with the lustful crowd.

"Onstage was a stripper named Chinadoll, who was giving the crowd their money's worth. She was a gorgeous Cambodian woman who stood five three and had a Coke-bottle frame and an ass like Trina. In her red satin lingerie, she looped around the pole with her leg and then came down to the floor doing a split. Fifty and hundred dollar bills paraded the stage as she fucked the stage in a split position.

Chinadoll came to her knees, flung her ass to the crowd, and made her ass cheeks bounce up and down. The voluptuous stripper was the only competition that Tameka had, and since Tameka was now her boss, she was the new Tameka.

"Baby, you sho' know how to find 'em!" Jarvis said to Tameka as they were both watching the show from the bar section, cuddling in their own zone.

"She's from Florida . . . an old friend . . ."

"She's from Palm Beach, right?" Jarvis asked.

"Yeah, 561, baby!" Tameka replied, emphasizing her hometown area code.

"Okay, Florida. Let's remember where only shit like this goes down!" Jarvis said, pointing at the stage where Chinadoll was slowly removing her lingerie.

Damn that bitch got more pussy than a man can handle, he thought while taking in the sight of

Chinadoll's waxed, hairless pussy. He was so locked in that he was unaware that Tameka was watching him.

All you niggas are dogs, she thought.

"Hello, I'm standing here with you, for God's sake . . . respect!" Tameka said sternly.

"Sorry, baby. But you're mistaking me for staring too hard. I'm more concerned about the money. I have too much ass to fuck over!" Jarvis said as he palmed Tameka's ass in her silk minidress that accentuated her curves.

"Whatever! I know that look, Jarvis," Tameka said, rolling her eyes.

When Tameka turned back toward the stage, she saw Big Dee walking toward her and Jarvis.

"What's up, player?" Jarvis said to him, pounding him on his fist.

"Everything money, shawty!" Big Dee retorted.

"Baby, I'll see you when you're done handling your business," Tameka said, giving Jarvis a kiss that slightly aroused both of them, for it was passionate and neither of them wanted it to end.

Damn, I can't wait to get home, she thought, knowing without a doubt that Jarvis was thinking the same.

"I'll see you later, baby!" Jarvis said, letting her go.

When Tameka was gone backstage, Big Dee looked over at Jarvis and shook his head.

"Boy, if Tameka ain't got your asshole wide open, then I know something . . . if nothing!" he exclaimed.

"Whatever, nigga! What's good though?"

"Our guest is waiting in the office, and everything is everything," Big Dee said.

"Good! Let's go check 'em out," Jarvis said, jumping off the bar stool and walking toward the back, en route to his office.

When he stepped into the opulent office, he greeted his Florida connect with a firm handshake, and did the same to his connect's bodyguard.

"So, Spin . . . what's good, ol' school?"

"Shit, son. You're the provider, and you know how players do. They play the game," Spin retorted, crossing his Mauri gator skin boots across one another. "I've been faithful, son."

"Most definitely," Jarvis exclaimed, shaking his head as he sat behind his ornate desk.

"I was wondering if we could increase our figures from the current figure," Spin explained.

"And what are we trying to increase?" Jarvis asked while fondling his goatee, out of habit.

"We're capping fifty a month. Let's slow down the traffic and shoot us a hundred. That'll keep us off the road for two months' time," Spin said.

He seems worried about the road all of a sudden, and one hundred kilos of cocaine is a big loss if anything happens, Jarvis thought, contemplating on whether he should approve the recommendation or refuse.

What would Benjamin do? he thought to himself before he answered.

"So, you feel that the traffic is becoming a problem?" Jarvis asked.

"No, son. It's not about a problem. It's about changing up the routine, son. If I can map out an individual route every month, then I will eventually be able to hit him for the come up. I understand that you're worried and have already considered the possibility that if something goes wrong, how much of a big loss it would be. But if I'm asking for it, then I could cover it all," Spin spoke with his hands. "Let's not forget we came into this business by washing each other's back," Spin spoke voraciously.

He's right. We did come into business washing each other's backs. But we had Benjamin put pussy before business and turn against the man who gave him the green light. I could trust him and prepare for the worst, or I could say hell no and not worry about a loss, he deliberated.

"How 'bout I lay on this right now and we come to a conclusion at our next meeting?" Jarvis told Spin.

"That's no problem, son," Spin responded as he stood up and prepared to leave.

Big Shawn, Spin's bodyguard, also stood up and then grabbed the two duffel bags on the floor, with his massive hands.

"Call me when you've made up your mind," Spin said, walking toward the door. "Oh, before I forget to tell you. I'm a veteran in this game, son, and I know how to access my plugs to their expedient purposes. When a man reaches that level, he feels as though he knew nothing of his plug. So he moves on, son . . . elevate!" Spin added as he immediately left the office with Big Shawn on his heels.

He had nothing else to say to Jarvis. In fact, he had no more money to spend with him. He'd tested Jarvis's heart without Benjamin's face upon the earth. If Benjamin were alive today, I would have had whatever I requested, Spin thought. Benjamin's death had already seemed fishy to Spin, but that still couldn't bring a dead man back. For him to be reluctant to accommodating my recommendation, it only showed me where we really stand as partners, he thought.

In all truth, Spin didn't need Jarvis's connect. He had a Cuban connect he had established down in Miami months ago. Jarvis was just another statistic on his list of enemies now.

"Big Shawn, I want this nigga removed, and I want it done clean," Spin stated while in the backseat of the Lincoln Town Car, which Big Shawn was driving.

"Ten-four!" Big Shawn answered.

8

When Champagne heard the mailman's jeep make its stops, she hurried from her room and walked past her grandmother, Ms. Mae, who was humming in her rocking chair. Ms. Mae watched her granddaughter closely, observing the pep in her strut.

What got that young lady all energetic? Ms. Mae wanted to know.

It was useless to peek out the front screen door, because her vision was poor. All she would be able to see was a blurry cloud.

Champagne waited until the mailman came down on her side of the street, and caught him at their mailbox. He had a big smile on his face as he came to their address.

"Hey there, lovely lady. You're on time again, I see?" Mr. Coleman said while handing her a stack of mail.

"Yeah, Grandma's making me," she lied.

"Tell her I said hello," Mr. Coleman said.

He was a very tall, muscular man with a dark complexion. He was in his fifties and had a shiny bald head, and he had had a crush on Champagne since she could remember, at just thirteen years old.

"I will!" she retorted. Fuckin' pervert! she thought as he pulled off to complete his route.

When he was gone, Champagne slowly walked toward the house and looked through the stack of mail.

Bingo! she thought when she came across Ms. Mae's SSI and veteran checks, which she quickly slid into her navy sweater pocket and walked inside the house.

"Grandma, you have mail," Champagne called to her. "There is nothing but bills."

"Did you see any of my checks?" Ms. Mae asked, wondering why her last checks had been late.

"No, Grandma. All I got here are bills . . . the phone bill and light bill."

"I don't know what's going on," Ms. Mae said.

"I will call for you, and I will handle the bills, okay?" Champagne said.

"That's so sweet of you. I will make sure that I give you the money back," Ms. Mae said.

"Okay, Grandma," Champagne answered.

She handed her grandma the stack of mail and then walked back to her room. Both checks were for $1,200 a piece, which would do her good for a couple weeks.

* * *

We're supposed to be brother and sister, and without Mom and Dad, we're supposed to have each other's backs . . . Shaquana, we don't have that. You've put an outside before your own blood.

The letter from Daquan had made Shaquana feel bad, because she knew that her brother was telling the truth. But he didn't understand her pain. He had no clue how their parents' deaths had affected her.

I love my little brother, and he needs me. Damn! How could I have been so nonchalant toward him? Shaquana thought. He needs me, and I've been a poor sister.

Shaquana was home alone. Maurice was in College Park handling business, and her auntie was at her own home. She walked downstairs from her confined room, into the living room. Looking at herself in the massive mirror that was on the wall in the living room, she observed how much weight she had lost.

Damn! I don't even look the same anymore, she thought, turning to the side so she could get a view of her backside.

Where did my ass go? Shaquana unfastened her robe and let it fall to the ground. There she stood nude, surveying her body and the loss of her sexy curves.

How could Maurice love a woman like me, and how could he let me get this way? Shaquana thought.

Still nude, she walked to the kitchen and regretted the moment she stepped inside, because images of her mother lying dead on the floor came to her in a flash and caused her to break down. She collapsed to the same floor on which her mother had died as she cried hysterically. "Momma!"

* * *

A couple of bruises on his face and a cut above his eye were well worth the beating that he'd given Jerome.

I could have literally killed him with my bare hands, and I was going to, if Mom hadn't been there to save him, Earl thought as he lay in bed on his back, with the gorgeous woman, Katrina, in his arms.

He drove straight to her place in East Atlanta when he left his mom's. He told Katrina all that had happened, and his feelings about his mother dating a twenty-five-year-old. Katrina had no input. Deep down, she felt that the age difference was not of significance in any relationship when both partners were grown. But she would not express her opinion on the matter. All she would do was listen to the man who had just made love to her like no other had ever done. Rubbing his eight-pack ripped stomach, Katrina wanted more of Earl's loving and to take his mind away from the disturbance that lingered in his head.

"Baby, I appreciate you coming to me, and I want to tell you that I'll always have your back. You seem special, and I want to keep it like that!" Katrina said as she climbed on top of him and kissed him gently and passionately on the lips.

He was a big machine compared to her petiteness, and she admired every part of him.

"Promise me something," she said.

"What's that, beautiful?" he inquired while looking into her eyes.

Damn! She too gorgeous! he thought.

"Promise me that we will learn everything about each other that we need to know after tonight. Because I want this feeling you've brought upon me to last forever . . . even if things don't work out as we may plan and hope for," Katrina said with emotion in her voice.

"Woman! You're speaking from the heart or mind?" Earl asked.

"My mind could be controlled, but my heart has a mind of its own when it sees something it needs," she retorted. "So to answer your question, I'm speaking from my heart, Earl. I want to love you and change you . . . and have you all for myself," she said, kissing his body as she slid beneath the comfortable cover.

Damn, this baby is . . . ! she thought.

"Aww shit!" Earl moaned out as Katrina took his erect love tool in her mouth. Instantly his toes curled into a fetal position, and his ass cheeks tightened up. "Yes, baby!" Earl let out breathlessly as she slurped on his dick. She had his balls in her hands, massaging them while taking more than she'd expected to the back of her throat, only gagging a little when coming down his enormous pole and stroking his dick.

She then lifted up his leg, leaving the metal leg extended, and began to lick his asshole. He resisted a little, for he'd never indulged in that type of foreplay.

"Relax, baby, and let momma take care of you," Katrina said as she calmed him down.

As she resumed licking his ass and stroking him, Earl relaxed. The feeling was great to him and, just that fast, Katrina had made history with him. She was the first girl that he'd ever allowed near his asshole. When she was ready to feel Earl's throbbing dick inside of her sultry womb, she climbed on top of him and slowly descended down his pole until he filled her womb and she felt him tickling her stomach.

"Yesss!" she whispered in a shout while trembling, before continuing to ride him slowly.

9

Maurice was in one of his stash houses at a low-key spot that only three of the men in his circle knew about. It was a plush suite in the wealthy area of College Park, and all the men were present in his circle.

His cousin D-Rock stood five nine and was an elegant high-yellow complexion gunslanger. He was in charge of the 12th Street turf when Maurice wasn't around. The both of them were joined at the table in the suite's kitchen with their two lieutenants: Coy and Arab Hajji, who the city feared most next to Romel's rep in the slaughter field. Arab Hajji stood five eight and most times went underestimated as a College Park pretty boy, until he had to make an example of someone. Coy, on the other hand, stood at the same height but was black as hell and had a golden glove in boxing. They were all in with Maurice and were ready to bring down Romel and Haitian Beny.

Maurice had been meticulous with his hustling to avoid the feds invading him as well as to watch his enemies closely, despite the tension among 12th Street and the niggas off of 3rd. Still Maurice had managed to make a profit. Now he was like a lion; he was tired of waiting for Haitian Beny's wrath and was now ready to bring it to him.

He knew of a couple of traps that Beny had in Bankhead, and was ready to lay down all the niggas who had his work—the famous whip. Being that

Beny had the streets back in his pockets, he saw no need to enhance the cocaine, because there was no competition. Benjamin was the last, and he had been easily removed.

Maurice had told his circle that Haitian Beny wanted him to assassinate Benjamin, but before he'd had a chance to carry out the mission, someone else did it. So T-Zoe was still in debt, something that Haitian Beny didn't need to tell him. What Maurice didn't tell his circle, for irrelevant reasons, was that he was sleeping with Benjamin's daughter and was in love with her—to the point that he was ready to die for her if he had to.

"So, Coy . . . these niggas in Bankhead stay in the trap twenty-four seven, huh?" D-Rock asked while putting a rubber band on a stack of hundreds and then storing it in a black Adidas duffel bag.

Click! Click!

"Yeah, twenty-four seven . . . and we're going to get them," Maurice said, cocking back his Glock .21 that had a red beam attached.

"Shit, I say we bomb them out!" Hajji suggested, ready to perform the traits of his country of Saudi Arabia.

"Okay, Bin!" Coy exclaimed.

"Seriously, check it tomorrow. We going to move on this nigga's traps and take everything standing and sitting," Maurice explained.

"Shit, I'm down with that!" Coy said.

"In the name of T-Zoe. We all down for some action. It's time to let these motherfuckas hear the trumpet of 12th Street wrath!" Maurice announced, looking at all his men in their eyes, with sincerity and determination.

* * *

Ppssttt! Boom! Ppssttt! Boom! Ppssttt! Boom! Ppssttt! Boom!

The sound of four Molotov cocktails smashed through the window.

What the fuck! Shaquana awoke from her slumber at the sound of breaking glass and a loud explosion. She could hear what she thought to be a blazing fire. Then she heard the tires burning out.

Urrrhhhh!

As the smell of smoke intensified, Shaquana leapt from her bed, for the irrefutable conclusion had settled in: The house is on fire. Someone has just set our house on fire! Shaquana thought as she ran from the room in a sprint.

"Maurice!" she screamed, but she knew that he wasn't there, or else he would have been in bed with her. As she got to the stairway, the fire was making its way upstairs, making it impossible for her to descend.

"Oh my God!" she screamed, choking on the excessive dark smoke. Her eyes started to burn as well as her lungs. Trying to find her room was difficult, and she began to panic, which was the wrong thing for her to do in the now life-and-death situation.

"Help me! Somebod . . . ! she attempted calling out for help while feeling for the walls, but she couldn't bypass the deadly persistent coughing.

Choking hysterically and falling to her knees as the fire thrust its way upstairs, she began crawling away from the heat making its way to her. The sound of wood breaking and the living room roof caving in made her determine her own fate.

I'm about to die! she thought as she continued to crawl through the dark smoke with her eyes closed, unable to open them due to the intensity of the smoke. She collapsed in the doorway of her room, unbeknownst to her, and passed out.

* * *

Big Funk and Corey watched from the parking lot of Pleasers as the fire truck accelerated in the direction of the house ablaze. They smiled, both satisfied with their work.

"Haitian Beny knows we're good at this shit!" Big Funk said puffing on a Cuban cigar.

"He'd be stupid if he didn't know," Corey responded while calling Beny on his iPhone. The phone rang three times before Haitian Beny picked it up.

"Hello!" Beny answered in a sluggish voice.

"I smell a boar roasting, I say," Corey said, speaking code to his boss and letting him know that the job they were directed to do had been completed.

"Get out of there," Beny said as he hung up the phone.

Corey looked over at Big Funk, who was staring at him while biting down on the Cuban cigar.

"Well, what did he say?" Big Funk asked.

"He said . . . get out of here," Corey responded.

"Well, let's get out of here," Big Funk agreed, starting up the Suburban and then pulling out of Pleasers parking lot. They exited onto the interstate, which would get them safely back to Bankhead.

* * *

When Champagne caught the news of Shaquana's house burning down, she immediately sprinted three blocks, until she arrived at her friend's house.

"Oh my God!" she cried out as she stared at the still-burning house.

A crowd of neighbors and folks who lived on the next street all watched as the house continued to burn and smolder, surrounded by the fire and police departments.

"Where's . . . Shaquana?" Champagne breathlessly asked anyone who knew anything, inhaling a bit of smoke in the air and burning her lungs.

"That poor girl almost burned alive . . ."

"Hell, we don't know if she'll make it," an old man named Lester said, cutting off his wife, Sonya.

"Where is she?" Champagne asked, for she was worried for her friend.

Before she could get an answer, she heard Brenda's voice.

"Noo! Noo! Noo!" Brenda screamed hysterically, running past Champagne toward the burning house. She ran past the yellow caution tape, where she was detained by the police.

"Oh my God! Where's is she?" Brenda cried out.

10

Before Maurice made it through the sliding doors of the emergency department, he saw Brenda and Champagne through the window, sitting in the lobby among other ill patients and grieving families.

The atmosphere was filled with pain, grief, and anguish from frustrated patients and crying babies. Brenda was a complete wreck, and all Champagne could do was hold her in a consoling embrace.

Damn! Maurice thought as he walked toward the two women.

Brenda's head was buried in Champagne's embrace, so she was unable to notice Maurice's arrival, unlike Champagne, who held eye contact with him. It was evident that she too was in pain, from the streaks of mascara running down her face from crying.

Damn! Please tell me she's okay, Lord. Please don't do this to me, Maurice begged as he sat down behind Brenda.

Hearing her sobbing made Maurice feel terrible inside and afraid to seek the news of Shaquana's condition. Clearing his throat and swallowing away silent tears that he could feel within himself, Maurice looked into Champagne's eyes, red from crying, and asked her, "How is she . . . ?"

He stopped to control himself from breaking down. At that moment, he realized how much he really loved Shaquana. "Is she okay?"

Hearing Maurice's voice for the first time caused Brenda to break down into hysterics.

"We haven't heard nothing yet," Champagne said.

"Maurice, someone . . . tried to kill my niece. This is crazy!" Brenda cried out while looking at Maurice.

Who the fuck is trying to kill my bab . . . ! Damn! Only one motherfucker would be on that shit! Maurice thought, concluding who would be capable of committing such a heinous act against Shaquana. Bitch-ass Haitian Beny. I'ma kill him.

"The fire chief said that if she would have stayed in that house a minute longer, she . . . would be dead . . . He lost three firemen saving my niece," Brenda cried out to Maurice.

"It's okay, Brenda," Maurice said as he grabbed her in a consoling embrace.

"Clark!" a doctor screamed out into the lobby.

He was a chubby, short black man who looked to be in this late forties. He searched the room, looking for the family of Shaquana.

"Shaqua . . ."

"We're coming, sir," Maurice yelled as he helped Brenda to her feet and walked her toward the doctor.

"I'm looking for a Brenda Davis."

"That's me, sir."

"I'm Dr. Morris, and I want to explain to you of Shaquana's stable condition . . ."

"Thank you, Jesus!" Brenda shouted, glorified at hearing that her niece was in stable condition.

"Come back this way, ma'am . . . so I can take you to her, will you?" Dr. Morris said, guiding Brenda to the back. When Maurice began to walk with her, the doctor spoke up, "Sorry, sir. But you can't come back here . . . only her immediate family."

"Man, I'm her boyfriend, fat-ass nigga! I ain't trying to hear that shit!" Maurice screamed at the fearless doctor, in rage.

"Sir, I will call security if you're not able to follow the policy," Dr. Morris explained, pulling out his walkie-talkie radio from under his doctor's coat.

"I won't be long, Maurice," Brenda said, touching Maurice's chest.

Her touch sent an electric wave causing an unexpected sexual arousal throughout his body. It was as if Shaquana was touching him and responding to his chemistry. Brenda was beautiful, and they had been in the same room alone numerous times, but never had he come to see her as anything other than his woman's Auntie.

"Maurice, she's okay . . . just wait and see how she's doing," Champagne said, pulling an angry and perplexed Maurice away, breaking him out of his erogenous state caused by the touch of Brenda's hands on his chest. The look in Brenda's eyes correlated to what he felt.

Please stop looking at me like that, Maurice! Brenda thought. Maurice broke eye contact on cue as if he could hear her thoughts.

"Sir, if it was up to me, I'll let you back here, but being that we were told that this was an intentional arson . . . means we must treat her safety with extra care. Someone tried to kill this lady, and apparently the killer is still out there!" Dr. Morris explained to Maurice.

He had no choice but to follow the rules, and he saw that being rebellious wouldn't make things different.

"I will let her know that you're back here, and send your love to her as well," Brenda stated.

"Please do," Maurice said.

"Tell her . . . I love her," Champagne said, feeling that Shaquana wouldn't care shit about her feelings. If you loved her, you wouldn't have fucked her dad . . . and killed her mom, her conscience spoke to her.

"I will, Champagne," Brenda called out as she followed Dr. Morris.

When the door had closed, both Champagne and Maurice sighed in unison.

"Well, what do we do now? I guess we wait, huh?" Champagne said, with hands crossing her chest, looking cold and in need of a warm embrace.

Looking at her in her pajamas and how her curves were seductively accentuated, turned Maurice on. Despite his ability to sexually connect with her, he'd been avoiding the temptation, not wanting to dog Shaquana and add more pain to her life. He loved Shaquana and once told Champagne to back away when she tried forcing herself on him two weeks ago, when she requested to see Maurice to ask for his help in restoring her and Shaquana's relationship. She wanted forgiveness from Shaquana, for she was lonesome without her.

Staring at Champagne, Maurice almost wanted to change his mind and let her put the good pussy in his life for the moment. But he saw her as a gorgeous devil, unbeknownst to herself. He was digging everything about her at the moment, with his dick throbbing, except the waiting part that she'd insisted they were doing.

"Champagne . . . the last time I waited to see the results of the aftermath, I lost a true friend. I refuse to do that and lose Shaquana," Maurice said as he walked out of the emergency room and hospital altogether.

Watching him leave, she knew by his determined walk that he was on his way to kill someone. The same way he killed Chad, she dubiously thought.

* * *

Jarvis was in bed cuddled up with Tameka while watching the breaking news, once again of the Clark's residence burning to the ground. He could never think of hurting Shaquana as much as he wanted to fuck her. So the move that Haitian Beny had made truly disturbed him. In spite of Benjamin's betrayal, which resulted in his death, neither of his kids deserved to follow him. He was still trying to pinpoint Renae's assassin, dismissing the possibility of Champagne being responsible, but he was coming up short of a conclusion.

"Who do you think did it?" Tameka asked.

Shit! It's obvious that it's Beny. Why can't you see it as well? Jarvis thought.

"It could be anybody who had ill will against Benjamin. I'm lost myself," Jarvis lied.

"It's sad that it happened . . ."

Grimy bitch! It's sad that you're not different from all of us who killed Benjamin, Jarvis thought.

Despite wanting Tameka for himself instead of seeing her with Benjamin, Jarvis was turned off when he saw how easy it was to turn her heart cold against the man who had saved her from her crazy boyfriend. Their relationship was based on an expedient purpose, to Jarvis.

Enough money and she'll turn against me too, he thought. That's why I will have to get rid of this bitch soon.

"I have to run and handle some business," Jarvis said, getting up out of bed and sliding into his Polo briefs.

Damn, I can't get enough of his adorable body, Tameka thought, admiring his muscular caramel physique. "When will you be back?" she asked while grabbing hold of the covers to wrap herself in the emptiness of where Jarvis had just moved from.

"Why you always asking me that?" Jarvis said, slightly agitated from her daily nose-diving into where he was going or what he was getting into.

"Why you feel that I shouldn't know? Last time I checked, you were the only one fucking me!" Tameka said, with a hint of getting riled up from his strenuous tone and manner.

"Tameka, what we share is sex . . . and the same beautiful home together. I will respect you in public, but we are not . . . ," he said, turning to look her in her eyes, which now had water in the wells of them, ready to fall down her cheeks. ". . . together," he concluded.

It pained her because she wanted a man to love her, and she'd allowed the potency of money to rob her of Benjamin.

"He was more compassionate than you are!" Tameka said to Jarvis, who didn't need to second-guess who she was referring to but still found himself inquiring.

"What the fuck did you just say, bitch?" he said while hastily storming toward her.

Damn! Why did I say that? she thought while looking at Jarvis's fiery eyes.

She was expecting him to backhand the taste out of her mouth and beat her until she was near death—something that her ex-boyfriend would have done had he still been alive. But instead, he stood in front of her.

"Tameka, I shared a big portion of wealth with you when I could have simply killed you. I gave you a business of your own to keep you stable and allowed you to sleep in this beautiful home that we share, instead of killing you. I don't owe you nothing that a dead man once gave you. You had a choice to die with him, yet you chose to profit rather than die. The only thing I owe you is death, because I'll never be able to trust your skank ass. If you wouldn't die for Benjamin, your skank ass wouldn't die for me . . . or any other man. Once again, I'ma spare your life, but when I come back, I want you and your shit gone!" Jarvis yelled.

Everything he said is true, Tameka thought.

"Do we understand each other?" he questioned.

"Yes! I will go, Jarvis!" Tameka quickly responded, sadly.

She then watched him leave the room and the luxurious $3.5 million mansion in Bankhead altogether.

Deep down, Tameka hated herself for what her life had become. Never in her life had she owned the preposterous amount of cash that she had in her overseas bank account. How can a woman with so much money be missing out on love? she asked herself introspectively.

She knew that what Jarvis had just told her was true; he had every right not to trust her. A single tear fell from her right eye, which gave her a significant understanding of herself. "No more tears, Tameka.

He caused you to lose something, so now it's time for him to lose something!" she said aloud.

My daddy told me to never let an enemy roam . . . especially in your backyard, she thought, smiling with a mischievous grin on her face.

"Jarvis! Jarvis! Damn it, Jarvis . . . You don't know me. You don't know me at all!" Tameka yelled as she began to pack her things.

11

"Was it necessary to damn near kill the girl?" Jarvis exclaimed, storming into Haitian Beny's study inside his $20 million luxurious mansion in Bankhead. It was 6:00 a.m., and the first peek of day had arrived.

Staring outside his study's massive window, wrapped in an expensive purple and gold velvet robe, with a Cuban cigar in his mouth, Haitian Beny had to calm himself down from reacting in rage at Jarvis's inappropriate outburst.

"So now you can't . . . !"

"Another insult, and I will have the tongue removed from your mouth, Jarvis!" Beny said calmly and sincerely, with his back still to Jarvis.

"I am not Benjamin, for you to talk to in any manner, and I've always respected you. So please have the same generosity that I have for you, Jarvis," Beny asked in his Haitian accent.

The threat was cold and very sincere, which only made Jarvis more tempestuous inside. I will kill this nigga like I should have done a long time ago, Jarvis thought.

"Being that we are understood . . . now what seems to be your problem? Why are you so riled up, partner," Beny inquired, emphasizing the word partner by making quotation marks with his hands.

It's a game to him, huh? Jarvis thought

"Why did you harm the girl and take everything they had?" Jarvis asked.

Beny turned away from the window and looked Jarvis straight in his eyes. An ancient ornate oak desk stood in between them and was the one thing that stopped Haitian Beny from pouncing on Jarvis.

"Jarvis!" Beny said, exhaling cigar smoke in his face. "Why must we go through this? I asked you clearly what your intentions were with the house, and you told me that you had no intentions with the house. Correct?" Beny asked Jarvis, blowing another cloud of smoke in his face.

I did tell him that I cared less about the man's home, but I never meant any harm to come to Shaquana, Jarvis thought.

He was stuck between a hard rock of truth and regret. Shaquana was Jarvis's interest, and that was why he was here in the next man's home, acting off of emotions.

It has nothing to do with the house, Jarvis realized.

"Why must you harm the girl?" Jarvis asked through clenched teeth like a raging pit bull.

"Fuck that woman . . . and every damn Clark in Jonesboro!" Beny exclaimed loudly.

Raising his voice prompted Big Funk and Corey to step inside the study behind Jarvis, unbeknownst to him.

"We agreed that Jonesboro was mine, so don't!"

"Don't what, nigga?" Haitian Beny said while moving swiftly until he was face-to-face with Jarvis.

"Say it, nigga! I dare you to say it!" Beny continued to scream in Jarvis's face.

"Nigga! You think I'm a pussy? Money change you too, huh?" Jarvis yelled back at him.

He so badly wanted to grab the smaller man around the neck and throttle him to death. But Jarvis knew that he would have to kill Beny if he ever laid a hand on him. The man had too much power, and Jarvis felt himself slowly converting to the wrong side of the field.

"We're partners . . . not friends. It's a privilege to have your own city in your control, shawty. But since you want to play Superman, nigga, we no longer remain partners!" Haitian Beny announced as he blew an angry cloud of smoke into Jarvis's face for the last time.

The disrespect had reached the capacity of his tolerance. Quick as lightening, Jarvis exploded and pushed Haitian Beny so vigorously that it sent him flying over his desk and onto the floor, where he landed on his neck.

The violent rage had caught Big Funk and Corey by surprise, which left them temporarily dumbfounded, which was just long enough for Jarvis to sense their presence. When he saw them, Jarvis removed his two Glock .17s from underneath his black leather and quickly maneuvered himself to a suitable position, with both Glocks aimed at Haitian Beny, before his bodyguards had a chance to draw their weapons.

"I'll kill this nigga. Make a wrong move!" Jarvis yelled effusively with death written on his face.

Damn! he thought, never intending things to turn out the way they had. But there was no way for Jarvis to retake his steps and come out differently than possible death. With that thought of the perilous situation, and excessive perspiration forming on his face, Jarvis aimed one of the Glock .17s at Corey, inching to squeeze the trigger and slim down the odds against him.

"What the fuck you going to do?" Haitian Beny screamed, sliding into a corner and wincing from the pain in his neck.

"Man . . . !" Jarvis said, not sure of what he wanted to say. "Drop ya weapon, Corey, and spin around with ya shirt up!"

"Man, I . . ."

Boom! Boom!

"Come on and make me, Corey!" Jarvis exclaimed, sounding like a maniac after shooting past Corey's head.

"Do as he says!" Beny demanded.

As bad as Corey wanted to rebel, he knew that to make a wrong move would result in someone losing their life—and more than likely it would be him. So Corey did as he was told, and disarmed himself of his two Glock .40s.

"Big Funk, do the same," Jarvis ordered.

When Big Funk lifted up his shirt, things happened quickly. Jarvis saw the house surrounded outside by what seemed to be agents. He never saw the red beam on the center of his chest, but his foes all did and smiled.

Boc! Boc! Boc!

The shots came through the window and struck Jarvis in his chest, taking him down instantly.

Before Big Funk and Corey had time to follow up and round off on Jarvis, FBI agents swarmed the study with weapons aimed at everyone.

"FBI! Drop your weapons now!" one of the men, Agent Norton—an agent Beny knew very well— demanded. As much as he hated the agent who had sent him away for twelve years of his life, he was grateful to see him.

"Get down or I will shoot!" Norton reiterated.

Big Funk and Corey immediately jumped to the ground and surrendered.

"So, I save you again. If it were up to me, I would have preferred to see the man take your life," Agent Norton said to Haitian Beny, smiling and watching his men put him in handcuffs.

"You remember what I told you twelve years ago . . . Fuck you, cracker!" Haitian Beny exclaimed as he was hauled away in handcuffs by two FBI agents.

* * *

The pain in his chest was a motherfucka, but Jarvis was fortunate to be alive and to be wearing the Kevlar vest that stopped the slugs from taking his life. The impact had knocked him out cold. Now Jarvis was awakening from what he wished was a dream and sitting in a dimly lit interrogation room at the FBI headquarters in Atlanta.

Damn! he thought, wincing in pain and massaging the soreness in his chest.

"It feels better than dying, I bet!" FBI Agent Norton said, startling Jarvis from behind him.

Agent Norton emerged from the darkness of the dimly lit room, with his FBI vest on and two Glock .21s hanging in his shoulder holster. He sat in front of Jarvis, who had been sedated by the paramedics who arrived at the scene.

Who is this George-Clooney-looking motherfucker? Jarvis wanted to know.

Agent Norton outstretched his hand and said "My name is Agent Brandon Norton, and I saved your life, Mr. Poole."

Jarvis just looked at the man's hand like he was stupid.

"I understand you're not friendly with the police, huh?" he said, pulling back his hand. He dug into his pockets of his super-tight redneck jeans and pulled out a pack of old 305 cigarettes. "Do you want a smoke?" he asked Jarvis, offering one to him.

This cracker is a fool, Jarvis thought.

"My bad. I almost forgot that you're not a smoker," the agent said.

"Man, what's up? Why am I sitting here instead of in a holding cell?" Jarvis asked.

Agent Norton erupted in laughter, finding the statement from Jarvis amusing, as he was intentionally trying to get under his skin. But Jarvis was a veteran at interrogations, and he knew the procedures well.

"Mr. Poole, we could go at this hard shell act all night and even tomorrow. I could have your ass thrown in jail and charge you with a PBL (punishable by life) . . ."

"Where's the phone, sir?" Jarvis asked.

"We don't have one," Norton retorted.

"Where's my lawyer?" Jarvis inquired.

"You don't need one," the agent continued.

"So that's how we're going to do it, huh?" Jarvis asked, with a smirk on his face.

"Mr. Poole, let me be straight up with you. It's not you who we want. Hell, I was hoping that you would pull the trigger and blow that man away. Beny . . . well . . . Haitian Beny has been my project to get off the streets for a long time now . . ."

"I don't have shit to do with your beef with nobody," Jarvis said sternly.

Agent Brandon Norton was indeed a George Clooney lookalike, and he was one of the best FBI agents in Atlanta. He stood five eight and weighed

165 pounds. His partner, Agent Clarissa Clemons, was a very gorgeous black woman in her early thirties, who was currently in the field on an undercover operation.

"You may not have shit to do with my beef with Haitian Beny, son . . ."

"I'm not your son, and I'm refusing to talk to you. Can you please respect my rights?" Jarvis retorted.

Agent Norton's iPhone vibrated in his pocket, indicating that he had a text. He quickly removed his phone from his pocket and read the text from his boss, FBI Director Bernie Scott: Scott, let the dummy go. He'll come back to us before we come back to him.

With that said, Norton stormed from the interrogation room.

12

Haitian Beny was upset and was ready to war it out with the FBI after the raid. Fortunately for him, he had been released on a technicality. But he knew they were still snooping and trying everything in their power to bring him down. That's why he moved meticulously at every step he took. Jarvis had really crossed the line, and he had every means of making him pay for it.

Putting his hands on me and pulling his guns on me and my men was a grave mistake, Beny thought as he was sitting in the backseat of a luxurious SUV that was bulletproof and jet-black sprayed. He was on his way to his low-key residence in Miami. With the feds watching, he couldn't go after Jarvis how he wanted to, but he knew somebody who could. Big Funk and Corey would have to sit this one out as well. Haitian Beny thought he couldn't risk his two soldiers, although he agreed to how much they deserved to take out Jarvis. There were times where one had to think for all, and he planned to be prudent for his whole crew.

"Big Funk . . . turn off in Tallahassee and stop at the first KFC, shawty!" Haitian Beny told his driver-bodyguard.

Corey heard the KFC request and awoke out of his sleeping state like a hungry bear.

"Hell, yeah. That shit sounds delicious!" Corey exclaimed while yawning and stretching his massive muscular arms.

"All food seems delicious to your fast ass!" Big Funk joked.

"Yeah, whatever! Food is food, shawty!" Corey replied.

A moment later, Big Funk had pulled off the exit, and Haitian Beny had seen what he was looking for. They were being followed by the feds.

These swines done came back into my life, and I can't let them win the war like before, Beny thought.

Beny became upset looking back at the black Yukon GMC. He wasn't upset at the feds; he was upset because neither Big Funk nor Corey had spotted the SUV following them.

Five minutes later, Big Funk and Corey pulled into a crowded KFC and still weren't aware of the Yukon trailing them

* * *

Shaquana was fortunate to make it out of the fire, despite being singed from the excessive heat cooking underneath where she'd passed out from asphyxiation from the black smoke. When she was being wheeled out of the hospital, she leapt from the wheelchair and ran to Maurice, embracing him tightly. She kissed him passionately and took in his cologne.

Damn, I love this man, she thought while kissing him.

"You're okay, baby! Daddy's been waiting for you day and night," Maurice said to her, wiping away her tears with his kisses.

Shaquana didn't pay attention to the new Dodge Durango that he had been leaning against when she was being wheeled outside. She had no clue that

Brenda and Champagne were waiting for her behind the tinted windows.

"Okay, Ms. Clark, make sure you continue to get on the breathing machine every day for two hours," Dr. Morris reminded her.

"I will. Thank you for everything," Shaquana responded sincerely.

"It's my job to revive my patients, but they must be willing to help themselves first."

"Thanks for everything, Doc," Maurice said concisely, looking Dr. Morris directly in the eyes.

"You're welcome, young man. Take care of that lady, ya hear?" the doctor said, turning away and walking backing into the hospital.

"I'm guessing that I have nothing left of a home," Shaquana said, looking at Maurice and holding on to his hips.

"You lost a home, clothes, and every materialistic item, but not your family . . . and friends."

"What friends. You're my only . . . !"

"Stop it!" Maurice raised his voice, with a hint of agitation that startled her. "Shaquana . . . Champagne has been by your side, day one, worried sick about you and helping Brenda get through this difficult time. Your aunt is devastated. Your friend is friendless. All she wants is a second chance . . ."

"For what, huh? To get close to my man and fuck him too? Huh, Maurice?"

"Woman . . . if that's what you are worried about, then I'm not your man, because you don't trust me either. We'll kill this topic. Your auntie and your friend are in the car. You don't have to say shit to her nor your man. Let's go!" Maurice said grabbing Shaquana by her arm and escorting her to the passenger side of the all-white Durango.

Once inside, Shaquana looked back at Brenda, and Champagne, who was crying silently. Without her friend, Shaquana felt more naked than she was underneath the hospital gown, but she just couldn't forgive her.

"Shaquana . . . Champagne told me everything, baby, and you have every right to feel betrayed and upset. But everyone is entitled to mistakes . . . and forgiveness. All she's asking for is for forgiveness and for her friend back," Brenda explained.

Despite feeling self-centered and nonchalant, Shaquana's heart was far from forgiving. All she could say to her hurt friend, which simply destroyed their bond was, "Bitch, I hate you!"

She then turned around and never once looked back or spoke to anyone the rest of the drive to Brenda's house.

* * *

Markeina and Romel had been together every day at a variety of nightclubs, five-star hotels, and restaurants, yet Romel still hadn't had the power to sex up the gorgeous redbone, who wasn't giving up the pussy like a hood bitch would do, without seeing his cash.

When he saw her high expectations and self-respect, it reminded him of the odds of finding a moral woman with her beliefs. So he began to take it slow with her, knowing that the breakthrough would be beautiful. She was with him when he did business with his hood clientele, even when he was unaware that she was with him.

They both were sitting in the first-class section on a Delta flight to Miami, where Romel was summoned to meet with his connect for important matters.

"So how long will we be down in Miami?" Markeina asked Romel while relaxing in his comfortable cuddling embrace. The two looked like a deeply loving couple on vacation who were excited to be getting away from their normal lives.

Romel respected the fact that Markeina accepted the way he got his money—from the drug world. He was working to be the next drug kingpin by the next presidential election.

"I can't say until we're there. Why? Do you have some place to be?" he asked her.

She looked up at him and pecked him on his lips with a wet kiss. "My place is with you, Romel," she answered.

Then give a nigga some of that sweet pussy and stop playing games, Romel wanted to say. Instead, he said "And I wouldn't want your place to be other than with me."

Whatever, nigga! Drug dealers and killers have no place in my books. There's only one place that you're going, Markeina considered. "I have to use the restroom. I'll be back," she said, rising up and sliding out into the aisle, with her ghetto-fabulous ass facing Romel.

Damn, he thought while watching her ass jiggle in her sundress. When she looked back at him, she caught him mesmerized by her naturalness.

Every nigga's weakness, she thought as she sashayed to the restroom, turning heads as she passed businessmen and other couples of both sexes.

"Damn, this bitch is going to kill me in blue balls!" Romel mumbled to himself while rubbing his irresistible erection.

Behave now, boy. Patience is a virtue! he said to himself as he lay back and closed his eyes, unaware of the federal agents in his vicinity, who were watching his every move.

* * *

"So, you mean to tell me that you're willing to go down the drain with your friend and get your girl involved? Where's your consideration for her, if not for the kids' sake?" Detective Barns yelled at Tittyboo, who was sitting at the interrogation table, expressionless.

Detective Barns was still trying to build a solid case against Daquan, knowing that what he had obtained illegally could fall through, if the judge ever discovered how he'd tricked Daquan into submitting a gun powder residue examination.

"Tittyboo, we know that you wasn't around when Daquan shot that poor girl and young man . . . " Barns said, letting out a long, stress filled sigh. "We need to save you . . . and you need to save yourself . . ."

Cracker think he could get me to turn state on my nigga. He must be on crack, Tittyboo thought while listening to Detective Barns's weak attempts to get him to turn state.

"Mister, if you know that I didn't do none of what you're alleging I've done, then why won't you let the judge know that and free an innocent man?"

"So, you're innocent. How about freeing yourself pal . . . ?"

"Get me out of here, please. I don't want to talk to you no more," Tittyboo said, invoking his right.

Fuck! Detective Barnes thought, letting out another long, stress filled sigh.

That's right, cracker. Ya going crazy trying to break a real street nigga! Tittyboo thought.

Don't matter how much time involved, I'll never tell on one of my dawgs, Tittyboo serenaded in his mind to the lyrics of Rapper Plies.

*   *   *

Three hours later, Detective Barns was in the living room, with his tape recorder sitting on the glass table.

"So, again, you're giving this information up on your will and not by force or any promises, right?" Detective Barns asked to clear the record of any coercion.

"Yes, I'm willingly giving up this information, sir," Shay said while feeding her ten-month-old daughter a warm bottle of milk.

"Okay . . . the night Daquan came to this residence, did you see Tittyboo hand him the gun?"

"Yes, I did," she answered.

"Did Tittyboo leave with him?" Barnes asked.

"Yes, he did. When he came back, he was all sweaty and scary looking. I could tell that he'd done something wrong," she lied to the detective.

"Did he tell you what happened the previous day?"

"Yes, he did. He told me that . . ."

Shay paused, unable to control herself and keep the tears from falling. She couldn't believe that she was helping the state throw away Tittyboo's life. But the detective promised her that he would see that she be indicted for accessory after the fact for having sexual relations with a minor.

I have no choice, she thought. I can't go to jail.

"It's okay, Shay. Just let us know so that you'll be cleared," Detective Barns said.

He'd given her all the answers on a white sheet of paper. The only thing that wasn't a part of the deal were the tears.

"What did he tell you, Shay?" Detective Barns asked.

Shay looked down at the paper and read the last and crucial reply.

"He told me that he held Cindy down while Daquan shot her in the head . . . and T-Zoe too," Shay said before crying hysterically.

Detective Barns let her continue to cry for a moment before cutting off the recorder.

"Good job, Shay. Remember . . . you're doing this for your kids and your well-being. I advise you to distance yourself from Tittyboo. Because soon he will learn that you're no longer on the losing team. Now go lay that baby down and come complete the last part of our deal," he said while unfastening his belt to his Brioni slacks.

"Okay," Shay said as she walked into her bedroom to lay down her sleeping daughter.

I can't believe I'm doing this shit, she thought as she tucked her daughter in. She was grateful that her other kids were asleep in the next room.

When she returned to the living room, she had on the sexy lingerie that Tittyboo had gotten her at Christmas, as she walked over to the detective, who was stroking his erect penis and watching her undulations lustfully.

"That's right, baby girl. Come to daddy!" Barns said as Shay made her way over to him.

She dropped to her knees with a feigned smile and replaced Detective Barn's hand with hers.

"Let me handle this . . . relax now!" Shay said as she then took his dick deeply down her throat, gagging every time she came down.

"Ahh, shit!" Detective Barns exhaled to the sweet fellation of Shay's superb head game.

This bitch is the best! Barns thought, with his eyes closed, toes curled in a fetal position, and ass cheeks super tight.

"That's right, baby. Suck this cracker dick like you never sucked one before," Barns moaned in ecstasy.

In all actually, Shay had never sucked a white man's dick. And to do so robbed her of all her dignity.

* * *

Champagne was up to her neck with trying to get Shaquana to forgive her. She saw that her heart was unforgiving and had made her mind up to move on, but Champagne had every means of making Shaquana's life more miserable than it already was.

Fuck you, Shaquana. I will show you how to let things go when you got it good, Champagne thought as she waited for the mailman near the mailbox. As Mr. Coleman came closer to her, his smile seemed to expand more and more.

Sick bastard, she thought.

"Hey there, beautiful! You're on time again, I see."

Yeah! For the last months. Idiot! Champagne thought.

Mr. Coleman passed her a stack of mail and grabbed her by the wrist, bringing her in toward him, startling Champagne.

"What are you doing? Let me go!" she screamed.

"Listen, girl! I'ma give your ass a chance to get it together. I know what you're doing. Be a nice girl and make sure Ms. Mae gets her checks!" he warned, blowing his hot halitosis breath in her face.

"Oh my God!" Champagne exclaimed, pulling away as Mr. Coleman chuckled and then pulled off to continue his route.

Champagne looked around at her neighbors and saw that no one had seen the confrontation, which scared her to death.

He could have done worse than what he did . . . and gotten away with it, she thought.

Champagne walked toward the house while going through the stack of mail. When she found her grandmother's two monthly checks, she pocketed them and brought the rest of the mail to her grandmother, who had the neighbors next door recording Champagne's fraud.

13

Arab Hajji emerged from the black Dodge Caravan's sliding doors and swiftly and discreetly hastened to the side of the three-bedroom middle-class home. He waited until D-Rock had turned the van around at the dead end and killed the headlights.

It was 3:00 a.m., and the traffic was dead as it usually was in this section of Bankhead at this hour. It was where the middle-class families resided, and where Haitian Beny owned a low-key stash house. Walking up the street were Coy and Maurice, who blended in with the darkness, since there was only one street light working and the others dead. It made it better for them all to maneuver throughout the darkness. Arab Hajji could hear indiscernible voices carrying on inside.

"It sounds like no more than three," Arab Hajji whispered to Maurice and Coy.

"Well, let's see how many neighbors we can wake up!" Maurice said cocking back the slide to his Glock .21.

Click! Clack!

"Let's do this!" Coy said while holding his already cocked Glock .9.

They all split at once, with Arab Hajji taking the rear end of the house where a screened patio was in poor condition, making his job easy to get to the back sliding-glass door. Maurice and Coy took the steps and knocked on the door like maniacs.

Knock! Knock! Knock!

"Who the fuck is that?" Haitian Beny's heavy year-older cousin, Boxhead, called out.

"It's me, nigga! Open up!" Maurice said, disguising his voice as if he carried a Haitian accent.

"Me who, nigga?" Boxhead said while peeping through the door hole.

Go! Maurice thought while simultaneously aiming his Glock at the peephole and squeezing the trigger rapidly.

Boom! Boom! Boom!

He was grateful for the ancient eye hole in the door, because the slugs ate Boxhead's face and landed him on the stairs.

Chop! Chop! Chop! Chop! Chop!

At the sound of Maurice's Glock, Arab Hajji let his AK-47 rifle rip through the sliding-glass door, and entered the home, taking the off-guard men by surprise. There were more than he had estimated, but successfully he took them all down, one by one. There were five of them, and Arah Hajji had the countdown to one.

Chop! Chop! Chop! Chop!

"Hey, man, what's up?" the Haitian man screamed, jumping from foot to foot like he was dancing when Arab Hajji fired the rifle at his feet.

"Open the door, motherfucker!" Arab Hajji commanded the terrified Haitian.

"Okay, man. I'll do—"

"Bitch, hurry up!" Arab Hajji screamed.

The Haitian man timorously hastened over to the door and opened it, stepping over his boss's lifeless body. Staring back at him was a man he knew well, but he was unable to do what he was told to do if he ever came across him.

75

"What's up? You looking for me?" Maurice questioned before striking the man in the temple, which caused his knees to buckle and his body to fall unconsciously to the ground.

In seconds, D-Rock had accelerated the van, stopping in front of the house. Maurice and Coy dragged the unconscious Haitian man to the van and tossed him inside. Once the trio was inside, D-Rock hit the gas and left the scene, with plenty of witnesses, who by then had stepped out from the darkness.

But no one in the neighborhood who'd seen the abduction and slaughter had ever seen the abductors before. Inside the stash house, Maurice had left behind a quarter million dollars. The money was extraneous to Maurice and his crew, because there the crew had purpose other than cash. It was about moving prudently to play in the bigger picture. And the bigger picture was now at their fingertips. Because they now had a reliable source—a weak link.

* * *

"Tameka, can I speak to you for a moment?" a stripper named Coco asked as she walked toward her backstage at Pleasers.

"Yeah, what's wrong, baby?" Tameka asked her.

"Well . . . ," Coco began before giggling like a teenager. "I want to ask you if there's any possible way I could pick up some daytime hours."

Coco stood five four and had a gorgeous pecan Coke-bottle frame.

"I think I have two openings, but I'll have to check my schedule to make sure. How 'bout you get with me after the club, and I'll have words with you," Tameka recommended.

"Okay, that's great!"

"Alright, girl, go get that cash now," Tameka said as she walked off.

Despite her being the boss over the strippers and second CEO of the club, Tameka still walked around in sexy satin lingerie, stilettos, and fishnet stockings. She was the diva and made it known every night that she was in the place. When Tameka walked out into the club's capacity from backstage, she caught Jarvis making an exit.

Bitch-ass nigga! she thought,

She couldn't stand to see him in her vicinity. It was all for the money that Benjamin was dead, and she planned on making Jarvis repay the same favor.

"What's up, Majik! You okay?" Big Dee said as he walked up behind her, rubbing his massive hands down the center of her back to the lower part of her hip, tempted to molest her curves.

"Yes, I'm fine. How long has Jarvis been here?" she asked him.

"He didn't stay long. He said he had to run to handle something," Big Dee responded.

"Let me know if he comes back. I will be in the office," Tameka said.

"Damn! I gotta taste that shit one day!" Big Dee said as he stood there and lustfully watched her sashay away to her office.

When he turned around, he saw Chinadoll clapping her ass cheeks, on all fours while Kelly Rowland's song "Kisses Down Low" blared throughout Pleasers.

The club was enthralled while watching the gorgeous stripper work her magic on the pole. When

Big Dee looked at the lustful crowd of men and women, he laid eyes on a gorgeous caramel complexioned woman who was observing Chinadoll's every move. He knew the woman from somewhere; he just couldn't pinpoint it at the moment. Looking at this woman, you would think she was Beyoncé's twin.

"Damn, I know her from somewhere!" Big Dee mumbled to himself. Tired of trying to figure out who she was, he made his way over to her.

Damn! She's killing them tights, he thought at the sight of her protruding ghetto-fabulous ass.

He made eye contact with her and almost lost control of himself when she smiled at him.

"Hey there, Big Dee!" she screamed over the music.

"Damn, I thought I knew you. What the hell you doing in here?" he asked.

"Excuse me! Last time I checked, I was grown, Big Dee!" she retorted.

"That's alright. I'm just playing. What's good, though?"

"Do you think I can kill that pole better than her?" she asked.

"Shit, the way them hips are looking, I think you could kill any good pole," Big Dee said, throwing curveballs at the gorgeous young woman, who was only eighteen years old but desperately looking for a suitable income.

"Naw, for real! Who do I need to talk to for a job?" she asked.

"Serious?" he responded.

"Yes!"

"Follow me!" he said as he led the way.

Champagne looked at him for a second and then let out a long sigh before she followed him to the back of the club. She knew the club well from when Benjamin owned it, and she knew that Big Dee would vouch for her to get the job. So far, her plans were working in her favor. When they made it to Tameka's office, Champagne held her breath before going inside, and exhaled her stress, releasing a sigh of nervousness.

You got this girl, she thought before she walked inside, where she saw Tameka talking on her phone and sitting at Benjamin's old desk—a desk on which she and Benjamin once made love.

When Tameka hung up the phone, Big Dee spoke up: "Tameka, I'd like you to meet Champagne . . . someone I've known for a long time now. She's seeking employment here at Pleasers."

Both women stared at each other like they knew one another from somewhere other than this first greeting.

This must be Benjamin's Champagne, Tameka thought.

"Nice to meet you, Champagne, and what a nice name. Will that be your stage name as well?" Tameka asked.

"Um . . . um . . . I don't know!" Champagne retorted bashfully.

"Well, how about Ms. Benjamin . . . you know all about them Benjamins," Tameka said, emphasizing "Benjamin."

Oh shit! Big Dee thought, finally realizing that both women shared a common ground. They were both Benjamin's play toys, and only Tameka knew of Champagne. Damn! Big Dee thought.

"Naw. I prefer to be called Cognac!" Champagne said with a smile on her face.

"Cognac it is! Come back tomorrow afternoon so we can get you put on a schedule," Tameka informed her.

Damn, this a small world, Big Dee thought.

* * *

Haitian Popa Zoe regained his consciousness for the fifth time and found himself bound with his hands behind his back and duct-tape across his mouth. When his vision had cleared from the dizziness, he realized that he was in an abandoned house that reeked of urine and feces from humans and wildlife. When he went to move his legs, he winced from pain around his ankles.

What the fuck! he thought. When he looked closely, he saw that his ankles were bound by a pair of razor blade cuffs, attached to a chain that was attached to a rail on the concrete wall.

Haitian Popa Zoe was a short, stubby man in his fifties, who had come from Haiti to assist Beny in his new stash houses. After twelve years in prison, Beny had come out with a master plan to remove all his American associates in the dope game and bring in his Haitian descendants. The niggas in the hoods were too blind to foresee his intentions. But Maurice was already two steps ahead of Haitian Beny's corruption and planned to kill the organization while it was still in its infancy.

Walking in his direction, he heard footsteps down a hallway adjacent to the bedroom he was in. He could hear the irrefutable sound of trash being kicked around and cans being stepped on. When he looked to his left, he saw a baseball bat and a baseball sitting next to it on the floor.

What the fuck is going on! he thought while he observed the newness of the bat and baseball, in a perplexed state of mind. When he turned around to the entrance of the room, he was staring Maurice in his eyes and began to tremble timorously.

In his shadows were three other fierce-looking men who had bats in their hands.

"Popa Zoe . . . that's your name, correct?" Maurice asked him while looking down at him.

Popa Zoe shook his head up and down, confirming that he was indeed Popa Zoe.

Maurice kneeled down and nicely and calmly pulled off the tape over Popa Zoe's mouth.

"I did that because you've been an honest man thus far. Will you continue to keep it that way?" Maurice asked him. Popa Zoe again shook his head up and down indicating his cooperation.

Popa Zoe comprehended the American language well and spoke it with a heavy Haitian accent, so Maurice was grateful for the abilities that his weak link had.

"Good! Because I would hate to kill you worse than I have in mind already."

"What I do, man, I do . . ."

"You'll be okay, man. Trust me!" Maurice said as he replaced the duct tape over his mouth and then patted him softly on his fat cheeks.

"Yo, D. You remember how our coach used to bat us the ball at practice?" Maurice asked his cousin D-Rock while picking up the baseball and Iron Sluggers baseball bat.

"Hell, yeah. I remember that shit!" D-Rock retorted, catching the ball that Maurice had tossed over to him.

"It went like this!" he said, striking the ball with his bat and hitting Popa Zoe in his chest.

Bing!

The pain from the impact of the ball hitting him in his chest was tremendous and took the air from him. Popa Zoe's eyes widened, and he groaned out in pain.

"Your turn, Arab Hajji," Maurice said, retrieving the ball from between Popa Zoe's legs.

When Maurice saw Popa Zoe sweating excessively, he smiled and said, "We're just getting warmed up, buddy," as he tapped Popa Zoe on his head cheerfully.

"Let's see what you got, Arab Hajji," Maurice retorted as he tossed him the ball.

When Arab Hajji struck the ball, Popa Zoe closed his eyes but felt no pain, as the ball missed him too high. Popa Zoe sighed, grateful for the missed shot.

"Damn! You suck, Arab Hajji," Maurice said, causing everyone to laugh.

"Let me go!" Coy said. He looked like he could hit a homer, which made Popa Zoe shit his pants.

Coy caught the ball from Maurice and quickly drilled the ball, hitting Popa Zoe in his chest again.

"That's the way to do it, Coy!" Maurice cheered.

Groaning in pain, the cuffs and chains began to rattle from his body, trembling terribly. As Maurice kneeled down and looked the old man in his eyes, he snatched the duct tape from his mouth, but violently this time.

"Uhhh!" Popa Zoe exclaimed in severe pain.

"All I want to know is where to find Romel." Maurice said. "And I promise, you'll die peacefully," he continued.

"Romel . . . he . . . come by every week to pick up his product . . . on 54th, at the green house on the right of the dead end!" Popa Zoe exclaimed, wincing in pain.

"Bankhead, correct?" Maurice made sure.

"Yeah . . . Bankhead!" Popa Zoe confirmed.

"What day?"

"Friday night at 11:45," he told them.

"Good job," Maurice said, reaching underneath his shirt and pulling out his silencer. He aimed it at Popa Zoe's forehead. "My word is my word. Thanks for your cooperation!" Maurice said as he pulled the trigger.

Tat! Tat! Tat! Tat! Tat!

"Today is Wednesday. That means we have two days to get his nigga. Let's go!" Maurice said to his team, leaving Popa Zoe's lifeless body behind for the wildlife to feed on.

14

"So, you just going to ignore me because I have nothing to say to that ho?" Shaquana screamed at Maurice, who was just stepping out of the steaming-hot shower, soaking wet.

"Pass me my towel," he said, standing in the middle of the spacious bedroom. Shaquana then pulled the Polo Sport towel from his rack and threw it in Maurice's face. She was beginning to get turned on staring at his elegant nude body. He hadn't made love to her since she had come home from the hospital. And he hadn't been home at night, only running into the shower and heading off to work, leaving her home alone to worry crazy about him. Maurice had moved Shaquana to East Atlanta to a luxurious suite that only Brenda and Champagne knew about.

As he dried off, Shaquana admired his elegant body and became moist between her legs. She was wearing sexy satin lingerie boy shorts and bra, and she was stressed from not having any dick.

"So, when are you going to talk to me, huh?" Shaquana asked, moving toward Maurice in an attempt to corner him. He could see the lust in her eyes, sped off from her, and then stormed out of the bathroom and into the bedroom.

Much as he wanted to make love to her, he couldn't break. He wanted to bring Shaquana out of her self-centered shell.

"Really, Maurice? What's wrong with you?" Shaquana asked in frustration.

"Listen! We've talked about what the problem is. When you come out of that state of mind that feels that Shaquana only cares about Shaquana, then we'll talk!" Maurice said while he put on a pair of Polo briefs. He then slid into a pair of sweatpants and a white wife-beater.

Great, he's leaving again, she thought as she climbed on the king-sized bed and sat cross-legged.

"When was the last time you spoke with Daquan? Do you know that he needed money for a lawyer, huh?"

"What money do I have, Maurice?" Shaquana cried out.

"Why not ask, Shaquana . . ."

"Maurice! I don't know what to do!" she cried.

"You have to come out of that shell and forgive. Brenda had put up the house before it burned down, just to pay Daquan's lawyer. She doesn't know what to do now, and Earl is out of her control. What could you do to soothe everyone's stress?" Maurice asked as he put on his black Jordan 23s.

"Baby, please . . . come back soon," Shaquana said.

"Call me when you're ready to forgive and let shit go!" Maurice said as he stormed from the room, grabbing his keys.

When she heard the front door open and close, she broke down and cried herself to sleep.

* * *

When Mr. Goodman walked into his luxurious office, he saw a visitor sitting in the comfortable chair in front of his desk.

"How are you, Mr. Holmes?" Mr. Goodman said, extending his hand to shake Maurice's hand.

"I'm okay, sir. Glad that you've made it possible to see me, sir."

"That's my job, son!" Mr. Goodman said as he walked behind his desk to take a seat. "Do you want anything to drink, sir?"

"No, sir. I'm okay," Maurice answered.

"Okay, son. So tell me what's on your mind," Mr. Goodman asked, rubbing his caramel bald head.

Maurice sighed and then rubbed his hands together while leaning forward and tossing a manila envelope onto Goodman's desk.

"You have a client by the name of Daquan Coleman Clark. Inside the envelope is more than what you've told Brenda Davis that you needed. I need you to bring Daquan home, sir," Maurice said standing. "Brenda don't need to know who paid the fee. Just tell her it's paid for, will you?"

Maurice then left Mr. Goodman's office with nothing else to say.

When Maurice was gone, Mr. Goodman sat at his desk a moment before he tore open the envelope. Inside, Mr. Goodman pulled out a legit overseas checking account that held $400,000 for the Goodman's law firm.

"Damn, son!" Mr. Goodman exclaimed.

An hour later, he checked the account to transfer the money into separate accounts, and started a genuine investigation for the defense of Daquan Coleman Clark.

*   *   *

"Markeina . . . now you said that you would help me with this tie!" Romel screamed from the bedroom of the hotel suite. Markeina was locked inside the bathroom, finishing up on her last touch of makeup. "I'm coming in a second!" she shouted back to Romel.

Despite them sharing a room and the same bed together, Romel still hadn't had a chance to make love to her. In the beginning, it was frustrating, but as she stood firm, the anticipation had built into a thrill. His sexual desire for her was worth the wait, for it would be a good feeling, like a cork being removed from a bottle of Dom Pérignon, he thought.

She can play hardball all she wants, because when it goes down, I'ma take her on a long-anticipated ride, Romel thought while sitting on the queen-sized bed waiting for the bathroom door to open and Markeina to walk out.

He was wearing an all-white Versace suit that Markeina had helped pick out for a special event that night to be held at the Marriott on South Beach. Haitian Beny had pulled some power plays to get Romel and Markeina placed on the invitation list to attend the event hosted by Spike Lee and Queen Latifah, who were presenting powerful African kings and inspirational speeches.

Haitian Beny was invited by his Cuban connect who many people called Cuban Black, being he was no different from an extremely swarthy-complexioned negro. Cuban Black had the streets in Miami on their knees, and he had a lengthy team of employed LEOs (law enforcement officers). He was a powerful man who the feds desperately wanted.

However, they had no evidence to tie him to the drug world and outrageous murder rate for which he had been suspected of being responsible.

Despite Haitian Beny meeting up with his connect and long-time friend tonight, Romel would never learn of Cuban Black and who he was, nor would he be lucky enough to be in the same room as him.

This Miami shit is what's happening. I got to visit more often . . . when Markeina isn't with me, most definitely, Romel thought as he lay back on the bed while simultaneously checking the time on his gold and diamond Rolex. It was 8:45 p.m.

Damn! We need to move it, he thought just as he heard the bathroom door open. When he sat up and saw Markeina walk into the room, he instantly caught an erection while staring at her breathtaking beauty.

Damn! he thought admirably.

"What do you think?" she asked while modeling her Armani Privé silk crepe gown in royal purple, which accentuated her delicate curves. She also had on five-inch stilettos by Jason Wu. Around her neck and wrist were sets of pearls.

She was beautiful and extremely titillating.

"Umm! Uh . . . you are?"

"Boy, stop putting on!" Markeina exclaimed with a sexy pout on her face as she walked up to Romel and immediately adjusted his tie.

"Do you know what that shit do to me when you look like that?" Romel said while inhaling Markeina's Pulse perfume and Dove soap scent post-shower.

"What make you hard . . . let me see?" she said while touching on his erection that was bulging through his slacks.

Smack!

"So, we teasing now, huh?" Romel said while slapping her on her ass.

"You almost got some tonight, but now you want to tease me for real! You couldn't save that for a better time . . . like fucking me rough from the back and . . ."

"Let's go now!" Romel said as he stood up and stormed out of the room.

"What?" Markeina exclaimed while laughing.

"Let's go, Markeina!" Romel screamed from the living room.

*   *   *

Thirty minutes later, Romel and Markeina had pulled up in front of the Marriott on South Beach, in a luxurious white limousine. The back door was opened by the chauffeur, a muscular, jet-black Bahamian man. Out stepped Romel, who then reached out his hand for Markeina like a real gentleman. Like the gorgeous woman she was, she intertwined her arm through his and then walked inside the hotel with her date.

"Showtime, fellas!" FBI Agent Norton said to his team of agents in the back of an unmarked pressure washing company van. They were parked across the street from the Marriott and had a visual on Haitian Beny inside, and most definitely of Romel as well.

Everything about tonight reminds me of twelve years ago, Agent Norton thought.

"Agent Clemons, can you hear us clearly? If so, let us know how nice it looks inside," Norton said into the earpiece of his partner, who was on the guest list inside of the Marriott.

"This place is so nice. I feel like a celebrity. Is that really Queen Latifah?" Agent Clemons exclaimed into her hidden microphone attached to her pearl necklace around her neck.

"Good job, baby girl. You're doing good," Agent Norton retorted back into his mic.

"It's not fair! I never saw Queen Latifah in person before!" Agent Knightley said while examining the surveillance on the inside.

She was a gorgeous five foot five Blake Lively lookalike who was twenty-seven years old, just three years younger than Agent Clemons, who was her best friend.

"Don't worry, Samantha. You'll have your day soon, I promise," Norton responded, calling her by her first name.

There were four of them in the back of the van— two other agents named Harington and DeGeneres, with four undercover agents inside the hotel, who were also on the guest list.

"Something tells me that tonight we're going to get some interesting discoveries," Agent Norton said.

"I feel the same. Look! There's Cuban Black," Agent Knightley said pointing at the middle monitor displaying surveillance of Cuban Black.

15

It was almost 10:00 p.m. when Shaquana decided to pick up a pen and paper and write to her brother, Daquan. She sat down on the king-sized bed, which she had never had the chance to share with Maurice. She took a moment to think. Here we go, she thought as she let out a long sigh and began to write:

Dear Little Brother,
Sorry that I've been distant lately. I can only imagine what you're going through. Daquan, Mom's and Dad's death really put me on the edge in life. I wasn't prepared to wake up and live life without them. I spend my days crying and grieving, which has pulled me away from everyone . . . even the new love of my life. His name is Maurice Holmes, and he sincerely loves me. Donavon killed himself, but before his death, the world was shaky with us. Come to find out, he was a homosexual, so imagine how it affected me.

Now someone burned down our home, Daquan and tried to kill me in the fire. I'm sure you've heard. I just don't know where my life is heading, and, Little Brother, your situation only makes it more burdensome. I wish you good luck, and I promise to visit soon. Until then, Daquan, pray and keep a clear head. Oh . . . me and Champagne stopped talking before Dad's death. I caught her and Dad fucking in his office. What a slut . . . and everyone wants me to forgive her!

Love always,
Big sister Shaquana

* * *

"This is great, Romel," Markeina said, taking a sip from her champagne flute.

"I'm glad that you are enjoying yourself," he retorted.

They were sitting at a round table among other couples dressed in expensive tuxedos and scintillating gowns. Queen Latifah began a comedic routine onstage, followed by giving an empowering speech on Black Lives Matter. It was a touching speech that she conveyed very well, in spite of her risibility.

"And people . . . I'd like you to meet an African king from the Zulu tribe. He's traveled across the country to share his insight on what can fix the violence among us and stop these unlawful law enforcers from their brutality. Everyone . . . meet King Kwame Mutulu," Queen Latifah introduced, exhilarating the crowd into a resounding ovation.

Markeina and Romel stood and clapped their hands as well. In the midst of clapping, Markeina saw a huge muscular man in a black tux come and whisper something into Romel's ear. Romel looked over at Markeina, who'd turned back toward the stage as if she saw nothing. When King Kwame Mutulu took the stage and settled the audience down by raising and lowering his hands, Romel excused himself.

"I won't be long. I need to handle something," he said to Markeina.

"Okay. Don't be long, baby!" Markeina said as she kissed him on the cheek.

"Is that a hint?" he asked her with a smile.

"Maybe. It all depends!" she exclaimed, smiling resplendently.

"I won't be long . . . promise!" Romel told her as he walked away toward the men's room.

* * *

Inside the men's restroom, Haitian Beny and Romel talked in hushed tones. Fortunately, no one was in the restroom but them. Big Funk and Corey stood outside and prevented anyone from entering.

"Today I got a call from Benzoe, and he told me that someone came and killed Boxhead and a couple of my men . . ."

"Get the fuck out of here!" Romel exclaimed in Creole to Haitian Beny, who as well was speaking Creole.

"Jarvis Poole. Do you know him?" Beny asked Romel.

"The new CEO for Money Green Records, right?" Romel retorted.

"Yeah!"

"What about him?" Romel asked.

"I need him out of the game. I can't touch him at the moment . . ."

"What's the problem?" Romel asked.

He was tired of being a hit man, especially since the dope game was making him some tremendous six figures. Soon he would let everyone know that he would be retiring from his hit man profession. Haitan Beny let out a sigh and then explained to Romel

93

about his encounter with Jarvis and the FBI agent invading his home.

"So, the FBI is watching you, and you want me to step in. How we don't know that they're watching us now?" Romel asked.

"Because I've surveyed the entire premises. They want to see me out there, so while they're watching me, I need you to lay dirt on this nigga."

"Where would I find him?" Romel asked.

"The studio . . . and make sure everyone there gets it . . . even Antron."

"Antron! Why?" Romel asked baffled.

"Because he knows something that he shouldn't, and I need him out of the game as well," Haitian Beny lied. But he needed Antron dead to throw off the feds when Jarvis's murder took place.

Being that Jarvis pulled his insane stunt, the first suspect in his death would be me, Beny thought while watching Romel ponder his thoughts.

"I'll do it!" Romel said before releasing a long sigh.

"Good. Now about our business. For this favor, I'ma give you whatever you need from one to eighty kilos. You give me the debt, and I'll clean the plate. So don't worry about going to 54th no more," Beny told him.

Damn! He really putting me in the game now, Romel thought.

He then asked Beny for fifty kilos.

"You have fifty, son. There'll be twenty-five already waiting for you when you make it back to Georgia," Beny told him. "After tonight's event, leave Miami immediately . . . and it looks like you've found you a real queen. Just keep her out of your business, Romel!"

"I will," Romel agreed.

"Okay, now. Let's get out of here," Haitian Beny said, flushing the urinal and then making an exit, with Romel on his heels.

"He's making his way back to you, Agent Clemons," Agent Knightley said to Agent Clemons over her earpiece.

"Ten-four!"

"How about that fucking tie!" Agent Norton exclaimed in elation.

I got that bastard now! he thought to himself introspectively.

The entire conversation with Haitian Beny and Romel was now in the FBI's hands and perfectly translated by Agent Knightley, who spoke several languages including French, the basis for Creole.

"Do you know how badly I want to storm the place and arrest him now?" Agent Norton said ecstatically.

"Don't we all! But let's remember the bigger picture," Agent Knightley said.

"Agent Clemons is doing a great job. You go, girl!" Agent Norton screamed into his earpiece, seeing a smile appear across Clemon's face on the monitor.

Damn! She's gorgeous, he thought while smiling.

* * * * *

"Bands auh make her dance!" Juice J's lyrics emanated loudly. The lustful crowd cheered as Cognac worked the pole. Despite her being ingenuous to the stripper life, she was giving the club more than their worth. She instantly became a threat to the other strippers by stealing the spotlight. The niggas were thirsty for the voluptuous striper.

Cognac had on see-thru satin thong lingerie with white leather strap stilettos, and she was turning the place out. When she did a split and made her ass cheeks flex, the money rained on the stage from all directions, including the DJ's booth.

"Bands auh make her dance!" DJ Spine said over the mic, serenading Juicy-J's hit.

I see why Benjamin was fucked up about that bitch! Tameka realized while watching Cognac's amazing performance.

"Jarvis is here!" Big Dee whispered in Tameka's ear.

When she looked at the entrance, she saw him walking into the club like he owned the place. He was sporting a fresh low-fade haircut and had on an expensive, tailored, cream-colored Armani vest suit that accentuated his muscular frame.

Damn, that nigga breathtaking fine and has the nerve to say fuck me, Tameka thought spitefully.

She followed his eyes to the stage and watched him remove his Gucci shades. Tameka knew without a doubt that he was getting a clear view of Cognac. However, when she saw his face turn angry, she knew that he disapproved.

He knows it's her, Tameka thought, smiling. Her smile faded when she saw Jarvis make a dash for the stage.

What is he doing? she wanted to know as Jarvis stormed through the crowd of pimps, players, and ballers, who all had cash to throw away.

As he neared his target, Jarvis leapt onstage while Cognac swung around the pole and squatted.

What the fuck you doing? Tameka said to herself, because there was no way that Jarvis would be able to hear her from where she stood.

She and the entire disappointed club watched as Jarvis invaded the stage, threw Cognac across his shoulders, and carried her backstage. Bottles of all sorts began to fly at Jarvis's back.

"What are you doing?" Cognac screamed as Jarvis took her backstage and placed her on her own two feet.

Tameka wasted no time rushing backstage.

When she made it there, she caught Jarvis in Cognac's grill, shouting at her like she was some little child.

This man has lost his marbles, Tameka thought as she neared Jarvis and Cognac, holding her peace for the right moment.

"Champagne, is this what you want to do? What's next . . . prostitution? Huh?" Jarvis yelled.

"Fuck you, Jarvis! Who the fuck do you think you are, nigga? You don't pay my bills. "

"What damn bills? Your phone? Because last time I checked, you were still living with Ms. Mae!"

"So what right do you have to storm in here and act crazy on me?" Champagne asked.

Exactly, Tameka agreed.

"Do you see Shaq—"

"Fuck Shaquana!" Champagne shouted out, taking Jarvis by surprise.

"What the fuck you mean, fuck Shaquana?" Jarvis inquired, dumbfounded at the harsh remark against her friend. He was stunned. "Champagne . . . you and Shaquana are like sisters. What do you mean, fuck Shaquana?" he asked.

"Well evidently we're no longer like sisters, and I don't want to talk about it. I've been on my own struggling since . . . since Benjamin left!"

Champagne expressed, unable to stop the tears that cascaded down her face. When Jarvis saw the pain in her face, he realized that he was dealing with the aftermath of taking Benjamin out. He grabbed Champagne and embraced her tightly.

Damn! he thought regretfully.

"It's okay, baby girl," Jarvis said as she broke down hysterically in his arms. He never saw Tameka standing behind him or the envious look on her face.

"Cognac, will you be okay? If you want, you can come back tomorrow," Tameka said, causing Jarvis to look over his shoulder and into her eyes.

Skank bitch! he thought.

"Bitch, are you out of your mind?" Jarvis asked Tameka between clenched teeth.

"Last time I checked, I had all of my marbles," Tameka responded sardonically, with her hands clamped on her hips.

I should have killed this bitch, he thought as he saw Big Dee walk in behind her, unbeknownst to Tameka.

"So, you hired her, huh?" Jarvis spoke concisely, with more than a hint of what he was conveying to Tameka.

It is all a game to her, Jarvis thought.

"I sure did. Is that a problem, sir?" Tameka said, being sardonic again.

"Leave . . . and don't come back. If you do, I will kill you . . . !"

"Fuck you, Jar—"

Smack!

Before she could finish, Jarvis backhanded her to the ground. It was so powerful that it made her black out for a second.

"Bitch, get out of my club . . . and don't come back!" Jarvis yelled out as he then kicked her in the stomach.

"Uhhh!" she yelled out in pain.

His second kick landed in her face, causing blood to gush like a water faucet.

"Oh my God! Jarvis! No! No!" Champagne screamed out, which was the last thing Tameka heard before he kicked her in her temple, knocking out her lights.

Panting from his adrenaline rush, he stared at her unconscious body on the floor and the blood on the bottom of his slacks. When he looked around, he saw way too many eyes and regretted the mistake he'd just made. He looked at Big Dee and couldn't tell by the look on his face if he was upset by how he'd just stomped Tameka to sleep or upset because of how careless he was to do it in front of everyone backstage.

When he looked at Champagne, she walked up to him and wrapped her arms around his waist, still crying and trembling, realizing that only a man who cared for her so much would react the way he did.

"I'm sorry, Jarvis," she sniffled, "but what am I supposed to do?"

"Come on! Let's get out of here!" he said, walking past Big Dee before stopping abruptly.

"Big Dee . . . when she wakes up, tell that ho to never come back . . . and to never let me see her in my life again!" Jarvis demanded. "Else, she will die!"

"I got you, partner," Big Dee understood.

Deep down, Big Dee hated what Jarvis had done to Tameka, but he also knew that with her gone, it meant that he would move up the ladder.

Damn, Tameka! he thought, looking down at her bloody face and gorgeous body in her satin lingerie. He couldn't believe how a man could harm such a gorgeous woman. Much as he despised abuse to women, it still wasn't his business to interfere. When it came to money, feelings were irrelevant.

16

When Brenda pulled up to the Goodman Law Firm high-rise, she double-checked herself in the mini makeup mirror. Content with her makeover, she tossed the mirror in her Prada bag and emerged from her BMW.

She wore a super-tight Alexander McQueen minidress that accentuated her curvaceous body. Her heels were spaghetti straps that curved around her well-shaped calves. When she walked into the building, all eyes were on her, like "no she didn't!"

Brenda's undulations were being observed by every lawyer and paralegal, including the lesbian receptionist, who was a young, beautiful blonde in her twenties named Ashely.

"May I help you?" Ashely asked Brenda.

"I'm here to see Mr. Goodman," Brenda said.

"Twelfth floor, ma'am."

"Yeah, I know. Thanks!" Brenda said as she walked into the empty elevator. When she turned around inside, she saw the lustful look in Ashely's eyes and shook her head from side to side.

"Strictly dickly . . . sorry!" Brenda mouthed off to Ashely as the doors closed.

Whatever bitch! I could turn your ass out in a second, Ashely thought.

When Brenda made it to Mr. Goodman's office, she knocked on the door twice before she heard him.

"Come in!" he said, already expecting her.

Brenda walked inside and locked Mr. Goodman's office door. She then closed the blinds. When she turned around, she saw Mr. Goodman staring at her in perplexity.

He has no clue how good I am about to fuck him, Brenda thought as she walked over to him seductively.

"Ummm . . . Bren . . . !" stopping his attempts to speak, Brenda forced her mouth on his and stuck her tongue down his throat.

With no resistance, Mr. Goodman capitulated to her

He smelled of a heavy dose of Jordan cologne, and his breath tasted minty as she kissed him deeply. She could feel his erection arousing through his slacks and growing stiffer by the second.

"Umm!" she moaned out as she felt his hands slide up her dress.

"Yess!" he said as he found her panty-less and wet between her legs.

She hated to betray Jerome like this, but she had to play her cards to free her nephew, and one thing that she'd once relied on to get her through was her voluptuous body.

"I'm going to fuck the shit out of you, and you're going to free my nephew," Brenda said breathlessly.

She slid down to the floor and unfastened Goodman's belt and then unzipped his slacks.

Damn! she thought while staring at his enormous love tool. Look at the girth of that thang, she thought as she placed him in her mouth.

"Damn, Brenda!" he exclaimed while watching her work her magic.

She sucked his dick so good and skillfully that she had his toes curling in his shoes. He had already made his mind up on whether he would inform her that the bill for Daquan was already paid up. What she didn't know wouldn't hurt her, and she knew that it'd have to be more than one shot at the pussy, if she did have to pay with this fine, superb head.

Before he came to his load, Brenda stopped sucking his dick and climbed back into his lap. Here it goes, she thought, reaching behind her and guiding his enormous love tool into her extremely wet pussy. "Awww, shit!" she exhaled, descending on his length, slowly filling her womb.

I love you, Jerome, but if you can't help me out, then a bitch gotta do what they gotta do! she thought as she rode Goodman's dick, slowly increasing her thrusting at every stroke she came down on.

"Damn, Brenda . . . this pussy will make me leave my wife!" Mr. Goodman exclaimed.

"Don't do that! This is business, not personal. So let's keep this strictly business!" she stipulated.

"No problem with that!" he retorted.

"I didn't think there would be one!" she moaned out, taking all of Goodman's dick—making his day.

* * *

"Daquan Clark . . . you have a visitor," the female deputy announced over the intercom.

Daquan was lying on his bunk like always, reading an urban novel by Silk White titled Married to the Streets.

Damn, who the hell is this? Daquan wanted to know, since he had no visitors since he had last seen his Auntie Brenda.

Daquan slid into his boots after marking his page in the book. He then walked out of the cell block.

When he stepped into the chatty atmosphere, the anticipation of the surprise visitor caused him to put pep into his step. But when he got to booth seven and saw his visitor, his heart dropped. He was elated to see her, and upset at the same time. He quickly picked up the phone.

She looks so different, he thought, taking notice of her weight loss.

"Shaquana, are you okay?" he asked.

"Yes, Daquan. Did you get my letter?" she asked him, with a genuine smile on her face.

He let out a long, stress filled sigh before he answered her.

"Yes, Shaquana. I received your letter a couple days ago."

"Daquan, I'm sorry that I haven't been here for you like I should be . . . ," she said before pausing as she tried to keep herself together. "It's been difficult for me dealing with Mom and Dad's deaths . . . !"

"Shaquan . . . listen to me!" Daquan began.

"We don't know who did this to Mom, and it messed me up as well. But we must remain strong and find who's responsible," Daquan said to his sister. "It changed me too, and it fucked up my world. But I can't fight and worry, Sis," he said.

"I know, Daquan . . . and I'm sorry. I've been in this little shell blocking everyone out, realizing that it's only pushing people away from me," Shaquana explained.

"Where's Earl?" Daquan asked.

"No one has seen Earl since he beat the crap out of Jerome."

"No! For real?" Daquan exclaimed.

"Yes, boy . . . you'd love to watch that, huh?" Shaquana asked, with a smirk on her face.

"Hell yeah! Two big niggas bumping. Did Earl run him off?"

"I don't know, but I haven't seen him at all!" Shaquana replied. "Like I told you . . . I was in my shell," she continued.

"So, what does this mean . . . that I see you out of your shell?" Daquan asked.

"It means that I'm out looking for the ones responsible for our parents' deaths."

"What's up with Jarvis?" Daquan asked.

"He's over at the club and Dad's studio. He hasn't been by the house, nor was he at Dad's funeral," she said with emphasis.

"Damn, how did I miss that . . . ?"

"Because too much pain in the way for anyone to take notice. Jarvis has always had a chip on his shoulder with Dad's authority. To me, he's a suspect, and my gut tells me that he knows something . . ."

"Damn it!" Daquan yelled, banging his fist down on the counter, causing a moment of silence from the surrounding visitors. When everyone saw that it wasn't anything but a sudden outburst, they all resumed their own business.

"Shaquana. I have to get out of here. So much has been going through my head. Someone wanted Dad dead . . . and knew something that mother knew as well. And that means that only someone close would know too . . . Jarvis!"

Shaquana thought the same at once but quickly dismissed the preposterous speculation, for she knew Jarvis also loved Benjamin like a father. "Now I see what's going on, Daquan. But why would they burn the house down?" she asked.

"To clear the Clarks out of town," Daquan suggested.

"I have someone for Jarvis. Just give me some time," Shaquana said.

The revenge for my mother and father will not go away until all contributors are six feet beneath me, Shaquana thought.

"Sis, be careful and smart. I will tell you what my lawyer is talking about when he comes to see me this week to give me all the evidence that the state is using," Daquan informed her.

"I got to help you get a good lawyer somehow!" Shaquana said while rubbing her temples.

"Sis! I have the best lawyer in Atlanta . . ."

"Who?" Shaquana asked.

"Mr. Daniel Goodman."

"I thought there were some financial worries?" Shaquana asked, perplexed.

"Obviously the tab was paid by Auntie Brenda," Daquan informed her.

"So now what?" she asked.

"We wait for trial."

"Thirty seconds, booth seven!" a female voice announced over the intercom.

"Okay, Little Brother. I also left you $100, so order canteen."

"Thanks, Sis. When will I see you again?" he asked.

"Give me like a month, so I can see what's going on, okay?" Shaquana said.

"Alright! I love you!"

"Love you too!" she replied, blowing her little brother a kiss behind the bulletproof window.

On her way out to the parking lot, Shaquana thought about all the good times she had had with her little brother. She realized that he failed to mention her weight loss.

Maybe he felt it would trigger depression or something, she considered.

When she got in her Audi, she tried calling Maurice, but to no avail—the call went straight to voicemail.

I wonder why Daquan never mentioned anything about Maurice either, she wondered.

She tried calling Maurice again and got the same response—voicemail.

*   *   *

Arlene McKnight was a beautiful dark-skinned, curvaceous woman who stood five five. She worked for the Goodman Law Firm as their lead investigator.

As she walked into the Juvenile Department of Justice building and walked toward the receptionist desk, Arlene turned heads. She was a male magnet who instantly changed the atmosphere. By judging from her personality and maturity level, most people would assume her to be in her mid-thirties, but she was only twenty-four years old.

"May I help you, ma'am?" the older black woman said to Arlene.

"Yes, umm . . . ," Arlene began, going into her folder to remove a paper. When she found what she was looking for, she handed it over to the receptionist. "I need to speak with Carla Woodland from intake, please," Arlene said politely.

"Carla, you have a visitor from Goodman's firm. Are you available?" the receptionist spoke into the intercom.

"Yeah, send the visitor back," Carla responded.

"Sure will," she said as she pointed behind Arlene. "Young lady . . . go through that door, take a right through the next door, and then follow the arrows on the wall until you get to intake. As you come to the doors, I'll pop them for you. I'll be able to see you on my monitor," the receptionist explained.

"Thank you," Arlene responded as she started the long walk back to intake.

Despite being told that Carla Woodland was available, Arlene still had to wait two hours to speak with her. The two women then had an hour-long interview, which Arlene tape recorded. An interesting revelation that would benefit Daquan tremendously came out of it, however.

"So, again, Ms. Woodland," Arlene said to the white woman in her fifties, who was the same height as Arlene but was on the hefty side. "I'm going to run everything back to you real quickly, okay?"

"Yes, ma'am," Ms. Woodland retorted.

"On the night you did intake on Daquan, you said that he never requested to speak with the detectives . . . and you're sure because you remember him being quiet, right?" Arlene asked, reading from her notes.

"Yes, that's correct!" Ms. Woodland said sincerely.

"And when did he agree to submit to a gun powder residue test?"

"From my understanding, he had no choice. It was done quickly."

"And no lawyer was waived or mentioned before the test was done?" Arlene asked.

"No, ma'am!" Ms. Woodland agreed.

"Thank you, ma'am, for your cooperation," Arlene said as she cut off the tape.

"I hope that he'll be alright. My heart tells me he had nothing to do with it," Ms. Woodland stated.

"The detectives had no right to continue to see him without his lawyer present," Arlene said.

"There sure was no lawyer around," Ms. Woodland told Arlene.

"We know. Thank you, ma'am," Arlene said as she gathered her things to leave.

Mr. Goodman, I think we've found our first loophole. If we could show the court that Detective Barns violated Daquan's constitutional rights to obtain the evidence against him, then the judge must disallow the state to use it in their case in chief. You go girl! Arlene thought to herself as she accelerated her Lexus SUV back to the Goodman Law Firm.

17

She had never had a man express his true feelings to her like Jarvis did. After dragging her away from the club, he brought her home to his luxurious mansion in Bankhead. They made hot, steaming love, both releasing years of built-up anticipation. He knew she was Benjamin's, but he had still tried breaking her spell at times, to no avail.

The perfect moment to seize her had presented itself when he saw Champagne stripping her beauty away. It tore him apart inside. She was more like a sister to him. He'd killed Benjamin because of being betrayed and Benjamin's threat to kill him—something that Jarvis as a man living the street life took very seriously. He lived off of two points as a principle—and these were things Benjamin himself had taught Jarvis: Never pull out a gun without using it, and never let a nigga get away with telling you that he would kill you, because you was giving him time to plot.

Jarvis was lying in bed watching Champagne sleep peacefully while he retrospected Benjamin's prudent advice.

I can't even lie . . . the man taught me everything about the streets, Jarvis thought, which was the main reason that he had been forced to eliminate him.

Or was it because of that skank bitch? his inner conscience asked him. I still shouldn't have put my hands on her. Shit! More enemies means more problems, and there is no telling how she would react. That bitch got to die, and it's the only option. Champagne must have felt him thinking, because when he looked over at her again, her eyes were open admiring his elegance. They talked about everything, letting feelings take their course . . . except who the killers of Renae and Benjamin were. It was unbeknownst to them both that the other was perpetrator.

"What's heavy on your mind? I thought you told me that you have the world now?" Champagne asked Jarvis as she slid on top of him and laid her head on his hairy chest.

"I do have the world now," he retorted as he slid his hands down her backside to her soft ass.

They both were nude and explored each other's body from head to toe. She knew his birthmark location on the back of his left ankle, and he knew hers as well in the center of her stomach.

"Will you talk to Shaquana for me like you said?" Champagne asked.

She had told him about Shaquana catching her and Benjamin getting their groove on and expressed to him how much she wanted her friend back. Shaquana was the only friend she had and was a sister that she would never have. Jarvis understood her pain, from missing Benjamin himself. But he would never express the fatherly bond that he missed.

"I will do as I say, baby . . . and will you get back in school for me like you said?" Jarvis asked.

"I will, but not public school. I'd prefer to do home school . . . with Shaquana."

"Listen . . . Shaquana can't determine your future. I understand your love for her, but being nonchalant about your future doesn't bring back a friend. So with or without Shaquana, you need to cover yourself and take care of yourself first, baby girl," Jarvis told her.

"Why do you care so much?" Champagne asked as she leaned up, straddled him, and looked Jarvis deep in his eyes.

Damn! She's gorgeous . . . and hurt, Jarvis thought. He propped up on his elbows and returned her stare.

"Because! I've wanted you from the moment you showed me that you were the epitome of a real diva . . . and Shaquana, though sometimes I wanted her, too, I had to choose. I chose to love her like a sister and one day be a man to tell you my true feelings. I can't explain the root of why I care so much . . . no doubt it's ineffable; believe that, ma!" Jarvis said.

Damn, this man is so for real, Champagne thought, speechless.

"I . . . I do believe you, Jarvis. Please protect this and continue to love me like you speak to me," she said, unable to stop the tears from cascading down her face. She would have never thought Jarvis to be as compassionate as he was. Feeling his erection, Champagne slid down and placed him inside of her wet pussy. When she locked her mouth on his, she let out a soft moan as she rode him slowly.

"Protect this . . . as in us," Champagne purred as she made love to Jarvis.

* * *

When Brenda stepped out of the shower, she heard someone knocking at her front door.

That can't be Jerome already, for Christ's sake. The interstate is forty-five minutes away, she thought as she quickly wrapped the towel around her body, covering her breasts as she descended the stairs.

Knock! Knock! Knock!

"I'm coming!" she yelled out.

That can't be Jerome, Brenda thought as she came to the door. Instinctively, she checked the peephole to see who it was banging on her door like a maniac.

Damn it! What the fuck do he want? she thought while sucking her teeth. She released a sigh, exhaling her agitation before unlocking the door.

"This better be—"

Before her words could form a sentence, the visitor forcefully placed his mouth to hers and kissed her long, hard, and deep while backing her into the house and simultaneously closing the front door.

"Ummm!" she moaned out, trying to release from his strong grip on her mouth. She lost control of her towel in the midst of trying to resist his stronghold. "I can't!" she managed to let out as he slid her to the floor and immediately placed his head between her legs and stuck his long tongue inside her freshly shaven pussy.

Damnit it! That feels good. Shit! Brenda thought, forgetting that Jerome was on his way. But the feeling of Goodman's tongue was too good to stop him as he sucked and licked on her pussy like no man had done before. She quickly capitulated and began gyrating her hips while burying his face into her plump mound.

"Eat this pussy, nigga! Uh! Yes!" Brenda moaned out in ecstasy.

Damn! This nigga can eat some pussy, she thought, feeling her climax on the verge of exploding.

"I'm cumming! Oh, shit!" Brenda said as her legs began to shake. "I'm cumming! Ohh! Uh! Uh! Shit!" she yelled out as her load came squirting into Goodman's baby face. As she came, he stood on his feet and unfastened his pants, letting them fall to his ankles. Goodman's enormous love tool made her come harder. Without any hesitation, he was back down on the floor with her as he entered her deeply with a powerful thrust.

"Ahhh, shit!" she moaned out and let Goodman pound her pussy in hopes of him beating the clock.

However, unbeknownst to her, she was completely lost in time. There was no way to stop the inevitable.

* * *

When Jerome pulled up to Brenda's house, he saw that she had company.

I wonder who the hell pushing that nice-ass Benz? he thought while killing the engine to his Lincoln Navigator.

She didn't tell me that she wasn't alone. She said she was in the shower, he thought while emerging from the SUV.

He looked at the luxurious white S-Class Benz and decided to step up his game next contract when he was going into the NFL.

I gotta get me a white-on-white S-Class, he contemplated.

As he neared the front door, he could clearly hear the irrefutable moans of Brenda.

"Uh! Shit! Umm! Umm! Beat this pussy, nigga! Uhh!"

What the fuck is this . . . some game? Jerome thought, smiling.

"She knew that I was coming, so she wants to see how I react. I should play fifty on her ass . . . !"

But whose car is that then? he thought as he turned the doorknob and pushed the door open.

"Uh! Shit! Goodman . . . !"

What he saw fucked his mind up. He wanted to act violently, but he held his cool despite his heart feeling as if it was about to explode in his chest. It took a moment before Brenda opened her eyes and saw Jerome standing there. Her mouth was wide open, but nothing came out, and her moans all ceased at once.

Goodman continued to pump away, unaware of the fluctuated atmosphere—and Jerome's presence. Brenda saw the pain on his face and the deadly look in his eyes, but there were no words or sudden actions to take away what Jerome was seeing. Shaking his head, he did the unexpected, and slowly stepped back outside the house as he closed the door. She was hurt as much as he was as the tears fell from her eyes.

"Arrghh!" Goodman groaned out as he exploded, pulling his dick out and shooting his seeds on Brenda's belly. When he saw the tears, Goodman mistook them for tears of joy from a good fucking.

"I know dick make ya cry sometimes. Good dick at that, baby!" Mr. Goodman said.

Damn it! I was stupid! Brenda thought. Devastated . . . she had no one to blame but herself.

"It's okay . . ." he told her.

"Leave now, Goodman," Brenda said sternly, with emotion in her voice.

"What?"

"Leave now . . . just go!" she raised her voice. When he detected something amiss in her change of demeanor, Goodman fastened his clothes as quickly as he had come out of them and hurried from Brenda's residence.

Something had happened; he just didn't understand, and he hoped that it didn't ruin their play time. That's all he was concerned about.

The bitch pussy is the bomb! he thought.

* * *

When Goodman was gone, Brenda showered and cried herself to sleep. She so badly wanted for everything to be a dream, but she knew the odds against reality. When she awoke hours later, the sun was gone, but the pain had gone nowhere.

It was one thing betraying Jerome behind his back, but he looked me in my eyes, and I had the audacity to continue to let Goodman fuck me. How has my life come so close to the edge? Maybe it's time for me to join my sister, Brenda contemplated while crying silently and contemplating suicide.

If I loved him, I would have found a better solution instead of my body . . . his body, she thought.

"Why! Why! Why! Damn it! Why!" she yelled out hysterically before she broke down in a storm of tears.

18

On the dead end of 54th Street in Bankhead, Benzoe watched as the junkie neared him on the cruiser bicycle. He could tell that he was a junkie looking for a quick come-up. Inside the house were three of Benzoe's workers, who were wrapping a couple kilos for a client to come pick up. It was Friday, and the only dude they would expect other than that client was Romel.

"Yo, what the fuck! You lost?" Benzoe asked the junkie, emerging from the darkness of the porch.

"Romel sent me, shawty!" the junkie said sluggishly as he pulled up on his bike.

"What the fuck you mean Romel send you?" Benzoe said, sensing something amiss.

Benzoe was a big dude who stood five nine and was built like a truck, with a swarthy complexion. He was 100 percent Haitian and a vicious hit man from North Miami. At, he'd been down with Haitian Beny, starting from being incarcerated with him while serving a bid in the feds.

The junkie straddled the bicycle while Benzoe looked him over. He wasn't a trapping nigga, so he couldn't tell you who the junkies were on the street. And no one but a few knew that this was the trap. So Benzoe's antennae were extended. But the junkie had mentioned Romel, and it was Romel's routine to show up on Fridays. The only problem was that Benzoe had been told that he would not be seeing Romel this week and that was from Romel himself.

"So, Romel sent you, huh?" Benzoe asked, skeptical of the junkie.

"Yeah, man. He sent me to holla at Benzoe."

"And what did he say to tell Benzoe?" Benzoe asked him as a car pulled into the driveway with its high beams on, blinding Benzoe. "Who the fuck is this?" Benzoe asked while lifting his hands to shield from the glare of the high beams.

He never saw the junkie come from under his filthy coat with the silencer P89, which he aimed at Benzoe's chest and pulled the trigger.

Tat! Tat! Tat! Tat!

The slugs immediately dropped Benzoe to his death. The car doors opened, and three men emerged together. The junkie hopped off of the bicycle and rushed the trap with the three men. When the first man sitting at the kitchen table saw the junkie with the filthy coat aiming his P89 at him, he shit his pants.

"What's up, T-man?" Maurice said as he pulled the trigger twice. D-Rock, Arab Hajji, and Coy carried the slaughter on into the living room, leaving no witnesses behind. Once again, the four assassins left a trap with double six figures behind. For money wasn't the essence of them; it was all about the takeover.

Romel will get the picture soon . . . the same for Haitian Beny, Maurice thought as he left the scene.

* * *

When Maurice stepped inside the quiet suite, he tried his best to keep from waking Shaquana, who was lying on the sofa in her silk pajamas. When she changed positions in her sleep, he paused and stared at her balled in a fetal position. The sight of her ass sticking out and exposing her pink thong instantly made his dick hard and made him want to take her by surprise. But he couldn't. It would only ruin his principle to show her how to stop being stubborn.

"Damn! Why do you have to be so stubborn?" he mumbled while walking into the bedroom. He glanced at the digital clock illuminating the oak nightstand and saw that it was 3:00 a.m.

Damn! I'm tired, he thought, releasing a yawn. But he would shower and then leave again. He stripped out of his clothes and laid his Glock .17 on the bed to gather his shower necessities. When he had his boxers and shaving cream, he grabbed his Glock and walked into the bathroom.

Too far to be slipping now, he thought as he laid his Glock on the lid of the toilet.

Maurice applied his shaving cream and then hopped into the steaming shower with a razor. The hot water only made him more tired. With his eyes closed, he shaved the hair from his face, giving him a smooth, clean appearance.

He never heard the door open to the shower nor Shaquana step in completely nude. When Maurice did sense her, he opened his eyes to complete darkness.

"What the fuck!" he mumbled lowly to himself.

Maurice became paranoid for a second, until he felt her arms wrap around his waist.

"Damn!" he sighed.

With her hands, she caressed his body until she found his manhood standing erect. Shaquana got on her knees and crawled on the tub's floor until she was in front of Maurice. She then sucked on him while stroking his balls.

Damn! I do miss my baby, he thought.

When she took him in her mouth, she felt his knees almost give.

"Damn, baby!" he moaned out as she slurped on his dick, with the water cascading down both of their bodies.

Before he felt himself about to explode, he pulled back and pulled her to her feet. Shaquana kissed Maurice passionately and then turned around for him while bending at the waist, saying nothing. Maurice entered her from the back, filling her womb with his love tool. He made love to her, allowed her to shower with him, and then took her into the bedroom where they made love until dawn.

* * *

The nurses on the 10th floor responded to an emergency buzzer going off. When they arrived at room 121, patient 2B's heart monitor was flat-lining.

"Dr. Randell is coming down the hall now!" announced a nurse named Rosa, who was taking the temporary lead. Two other female nurses attempted to revive the patient's heart, but to no avail.

The paddles were useless. They could only pray for hope.

Beeeeeeeeeep!

The heart monitor buzzed—the patient was flatlining.

When Dr. Randell arrived, he saw the nurses trying their best to revive the patient's heart.

"Come on, mama. Don't leave us today!" the doctor exclaimed, grabbing the defibrillator himself. "How long?" he asked.

Shock! Shock! Shock!

"Ten minutes, so far . . . 8:20 a.m.," Nurse Rosa said.

Damn it! Dr. Randell thought. Too long!

Shock! Shock! Shock!

"Second attempt to revive unsuccessful. Document."

"Got it, sir," Nurse Rosa said as she followed orders.

He let ten seconds pass and then tried again.

Shock! Shock! Shock!

"Come on, lady! Come back!" Dr. Randell begged.

"Third attempt to revive patient 2B unsuccessful. Document time of death . . . 8:30 a.m. Patient name is Pearl Susan Davis," Dr. Randell exclaimed to the nurse, who documented the procedures.

Beeeeeeeeeep!

* * *

Romel awoke to his iPhone's ringtone of Yo Gotti's Down in the DM. When he looked beside him, hoping to find Markeina asleep, he saw an empty space.

Where the hell she at? Probably in the bathroom, Romel thought as he grabbed his phone from the nightstand.

"Hello!" he answered without checking the caller ID.

"Where are you?" Haitian Beny said in Creole.

"I'm home. What's up?" Romel asked as he sat up out of bed en route to the bathroom.

"I don't know who it is, but I just got word that someone killed everything on 54th!"

"Get the fuck out of here, man!" Romel exclaimed in disbelief.

"Man, I'm still in Miami. I need those niggas Jarvis and Maurice history. I'll be there in a couple days," Haitian Beny said.

"I got you. Let me check the traps out, feel me?" Romel said.

"Listen, whoever it is, they leaving money and the product behind . . ."

"What do you mean?" Romel asked, bewildered.

"Romel! Whoever's hitting my people, they leaving everything behind. They're only concerned with death. I need both of them out of the way," Beny explained.

"I got you. Say no more . . . !"

"No, let's not lose no more," Beny said as he hung up the phone.

As Romel relieved himself in the bathroom, his mind went many places—but mostly to Markeina.

* * *

Across the street, Agents Clemons and Norton had just listened to Romel and Haitian Beny's entire conversation.

"So what do you think, Clemons?" Norton asked.

"I think it's Maurice . . . so we put surveillance on him and see for ourselves," Agent Clemons said from the passenger side of the unmarked Yukon in the parking lot of Paradise Palace in East Atlanta, where Romel's low-key suite was located.

"We're getting closer . . . that I can tell you!" Agent Clemons said.

She was as ready as Agent Norton was to bring Romel and Haitian Beny down. She had zero tolerance for drug dealers and murderers, especially after losing both of her parents to heroin overdoses. So in her book, every drug dealer was a coward and an inconsiderate, self-centered bastard. She was only thirty but looked twenty, and she had most veterans with the bureau outsmarted with her brilliancy.

"FBI Director Tom Channels wants to join the operation to see if we can bring Cuban Black down as well . . ."

"We'll never get Cuban Black to incriminate himself without getting close to Haitian Beny. And Romel will never meet Cuban Black on Beny's clock," Agent Clemons said as her iPhone rang.

When she looked at the caller ID and saw who it was, she looked over at her partner.

"It's him!" she said, giving Agent Norton a moment to connect the recording device.

"Ready?" she said laughing.

"Yeah!" he retorted with a sigh.

"Hello, are you lonely?" Agent Clemons said to the caller seductively.

"More like horny," the caller replied.

* * *

When Brenda called Shaquana to tell her the news that her grandmother had passed away, Shaquana didn't know whether to cry or smile for the lady she knew to be so surly to everyone, including her kids and grandkids. Brenda took it hard, for she knew her mother better than anyone, other than her lost twin.

To help Brenda get through the process, Shaquana and Maurice showed up at her place and were surprised to see Earl and his girlfriend, Katrina, there as well. The many folks that knew Ms. Pearl Davis had stopped by with their condolences and left flowers and sympathy cards. Earl's army friend showed up with his wife, Ellean, who was pregnant with their first child. Everyone then heard the story of how Charles and Earl had saved each other during an attack on them by the Iraqis. No one could tell you how the Coleman barbecue grill came out, but the delicious ribs and chicken left everyone wanting more. Earl and Charles put their feet in the grill, making the meat fall off the bones.

Brenda and Shaquana were in the kitchen and realized how much time had gone by since their last family get-together. Both of them stood at the sink and watched the party on the patio while darkness continued to fall.

"So, when will we tell Daquan?" Shaquana asked while rinsing plates as Brenda hand-washed the dirty dishes.

"When was the last time you saw him?" Brenda asked.

"Last week," Shaquana said, surprising her aunt.

"Really? And was he glad to see his sister?"

"Yeah, he was!" Shaquana retorted. "I left him some money on his books . . ."

"That's wonderful," Brenda said, passing Shaquana the finished plates to be rinsed.

Shaquana sighed and then looked her Auntie in her eyes.

"What do you think is going to happen with Daquan?"

"Well, I can tell you this . . . that he has a fine lawyer."

"Daquan said you've paid for everything. How did you do it, if the house is ruined?" Shaquan inquired.

"Auntie got her connects too, girl!" Brenda retorted. "I think Daquan will be fine . . ."

"Will he go to prison, you think?" Shaquana asked.

"Baby, I pray that he don't. If he has to go, as long as the Lord allows him a chance to come back home, I'm sure Daquan wouldn't worry himself," Brenda said.

"What will happen to Tittyboo?" Shaquana then asked.

"I can't speak on nobody else's child but my nephew, and that's all we should be worried about," Brenda said, hugging her niece.

"What do you think about Jarvis's behavior lately? It's like he knows something that no one else knows," Shaquana said, causing Brenda to pull her back and look into her eyes.

"You too, huh?" Brenda exclaimed.

"You too . . . what?"

"You sense something fishy about him. He hasn't even been around, and he didn't go to the funeral. I've been wanting to say something, but I didn't want to insinuate wrong," Brenda explained.

"He has all my dad's businesses and never bothered to offer anyone related to my dad at least half of his fortune. The club and the studio should have been ours!"

"Shaquana . . . Benjamin was a smart man. He left money somewhere, but no one knows."

"Oh my God! I never thought about that!" Shaquana said, disturbed by the new revelation. "I was too stuck in my shell to even think of the strong possibility of there being cash lying around."

"In time, things will reveal themselves," Brenda suggested.

"That's what Mom always said," Shaquana said.

"Auntie . . . I'ma go back to school and find the person who killed my father and mother. And when I do, I'ma make them pay with their souls as well," Shaquana told her.

"What's on your mind?" Brenda asked.

"Law! But I don't know which agency," Shaquana responded.

"What about cosmetology? I thought that was your interest," Brenda asked.

"That can't free my brother or find out who killed my parents!"

19

When Daquan walked into the attorney-client room, he saw this lawyer and a gorgeous dark-skinned woman sitting beside him at a round table.

"How are you doing, Daquan?" Mr. Goodman said as he stood up and extended his hand to Daquan.

"I'm okay. Just happy to see you," Daquan retorted while shaking his lawyer's hand.

"Daquan, I'd like you to meet my investigator, Arlene McKnight . . . !"

"Pleasure to meet you," he responded as he softly shook her delicate hand.

"Well, son. I want to bring you up to speed on your case," Goodman said, reaching into his black briefcase to retrieve a large manila envelope that he slid across the table to Daquan. "The reason why you haven't heard from me sooner was because of financial difficulties . . . um . . . when your dad suddenly died. At the time, he only hired me for your juvenile procedure. Um . . . he only paid $45,000 at the time, so I really had to wait and see if I'd be going forward and representing you. Until your Auntie . . . what's her name again?" Mr. Goodman pretended not to recall.

"Brenda!" Daquan said.

"Yeah, that's right! Brenda Davis. Is that correct?"

"Yes, sir," Daquan retorted.

"Okay, well everything's paid for!" he said, his long arms outstretched.

"How much?" Daquan asked.

"How much what?" Mr. Goodman responded.

"How much did my family pay you?" Daquan asked.

"$145,000!" Mr. Goodman said in his smooth Keith Sweat voice.

"Are you paid in full?" Daquan asked.

"Correct!" Goodman responded.

Where the fuck did Auntie get that money from? Daquan thought.

"So, what are my chances at going home?" Daquan asked his attorney while staring at the gorgeous woman who said nothing.

"Well, son, your prosecutor is a black man named Matthew Brooks, and he is the best in Atlanta. I've defeated him twice. And your judge is Kenny Stuart . . . Honorable Judge Kenny Stuart at that! And I've been in front of him twice. To me, he is . . . um . . . a fair judge; although, he is a white man," Mr. Goodman explained. "Everything the state will be using against you, Daquan, is in that envelope, son. Okay, let's get to the good part."

What's good about fighting for my life? Daquan thought to himself.

Mr. Goodman looked at Arlene, and she spoke after a nod. "Daquan, I went out to the Juvenile Department of Justice a couple days ago and spoke with a woman in intake named Carla Woodland . . ."

"I remember her. What's up?" Daquan asked the gorgeous woman who had a sexy voice as well.

"Well, it's important for the defense to know how you ended up taking a gun powder residue test after you refused to talk to the detectives . . ."

"I don't recall taking any test for gun powder residue, miss!" Daquan said truthfully.

Both his lawyer and the investigator looked at each other. What perplexed Daquan more than the smile appearing on the woman's face was the silence. What the fuck is she smiling for? Daquan wanted to know.

She went inside her briefcase and pulled out a yellow folder. She swiftly opened the folder, simultaneously sliding it in front of Daquan.

"Is that your signature, Daquan?" she asked, pointing to a yellow highlighted line with Daquan's signature dated March 12.

"Yeah, that's my signature, but I still can't recall taking a gun residue test . . ."

"Daquan, the detectives that your dad told you not to talk to . . . did they fingerprint you?" Mr. Goodman asked.

Daquan took a moment to recall.

"Yeah . . . at the juvenile center in a room. Then they left. Before they left, I signed that paper," Daquan said while pointing at the residue form.

"When he told you to sign, what did he say?" Mr. Goodman asked while crossing his long legs and leaning back in his seat, with his hands interlocked behind his bald head.

"He told me that I was signing orientation papers," Dasquan answered. Damn, I see what's going on now, Daquan thought. "They set me up, huh?" Daquan said to his lawyer.

"Daquan . . . listen to me good, son!" Mr. Goodman began, uncrossing his legs. He then leaned over the table, closer to Daquan. The look on his face was serious, and Daquan felt that he was about to be let in on a secret that no one was supposed to know about, other than the three of them in the room.

"Son, your dad is on tape telling these detectives that he didn't want you talking to them—period!" Mr. Goodman began, gesturing with his hand and cutting a line in the air. "These motherfuckers get you to the juvenile center and force you to submit a residue test, unbeknownst to you, because you don't know shit about it. So there is a problem, because before any other communication they want to do, the motherfuckers have to have a lawyer present to establish re-initiation, son," Mr. Goodman continued. "Did you tell them you would take this test, son?" Mr. Goodman asked.

"No, sir," Daquan retorted.

"The test came back positive, which made them go get a search warrant for your home, where they stumbled across the murder weapon with you and your homeboy's prints."

So, how the fuck will I get out of this shit? he wanted to know.

"You're probably wondering how, huh . . . how will Mr. Goodman defeat Brooks in trial, huh?" he said. "Well, if I couldn't beat him, I'd tell you, son, and see what type of plea deal that we could get for you." Mr. Goodman then paused for a minute before continuing: "Well, son, I can . . . and will . . . beat him. I can promise you that . . . !"

"But they have a gun, sir. How can you promise me?" Daquan wanted to know.

"When I get done with these dirty detectives, there will be no gun!" Mr. Goodman told him.

Part of Daquan wanted to trust Mr. Goodman, but he could only be performing for the money.

Only time will tell who he really is, Daquan thought.

"Trust me, son . . ."

"I have no choice. You're paid in full already," Daquan said.

* * *

Back in his cell, he looked over the state's evidence while his new cellmate walked in and out of the cell. What he saw hurt him to his soul. He stared at a photo of the murder weapon, which the state was hoping to bring into exhibit to convict him. Then he read statements made by Tittyboo's girlfriend, Shay.

This bitch is a state witness and is lying her ass off just to save herself from going down for messing with a minor. It's a shame what a bitch will do to sell her damn soul! Daquan thought as he continued to read Shay's lengthy statement. I got to get at Shaquana and let her know about this pussy-ass ho.

When he continued to read others' statements, he was shocked to see that a lot of people who he thought were solid were not.

I only have me and my sister in this crazy-ass world. Lord, please spare me on this one. I promise to leave all fuck niggas alone, Daquan reflected.

Not wanting to read any more, he placed the papers back inside the envelope and kicked back on his bunk to resume reading an urban novel by Jacob Spears entitled Childhood Sweethearts II.

I like that bitch China, Daquana thought.

* * *

When Tameka touched down in Miami, two of Haitian Beny's men had picked her up. She could tell they were simply straight up Haitian boys, not

Beny's bodyguards Big Funk or Corey. Neither of the menacing-looking men said anything to her on the ride out to the wealthy neighborhood in Miami Gardens. She was in the backseat of a luxurious limo and planned on staying no longer than a day. As they pulled into a gated community, she took in all the wealth.

Haitian Beny was a smart man to buy a mansion in this area. It is definitely low-key, she thought as they slowed down when they came upon a closed gate.

The driver let down his window and pressed the call button.

"Who is it?" Haitian Beny asked in Creole.

The man replied in Creole, and a moment later the gate rolled open to let the limousine pass through. Tameka was awestruck when she stared at the mansion . . . and at that moment, she fell in love with Miami.

Tameka was there to see how much Haitian Beny really wanted Jarvis dead. Because if he wanted him dead as much as she did, she would be willing to help him out, without any problem.

When the back doors opened, Tameka stepped out into the beautiful Miami sun and took in the warming hospitality. When she looked at the front door, she saw Haitian Beny walking through it with two gorgeous Cuban women, dressed in yellow bikinis, on each of his arms.

"So, this is what they call paradise, huh?" Tameka called out with a smile on her face as she neared him.

She kissed him on both cheeks like he was a noble king, and he gently kissed her hand like she was a noble queen.

"Glad to see that you've made it, Tameka," Beny said in a heavy accent.

"Me too!" she retorted.

"Come, now," Beny said, escorting Tameka inside and giving her a tour of his home. It wasn't long before Tameka hit Haitian Beny with her purpose of coming to see him. After she told him of how Jarvis had completely turned against her, he was sure that he had the right solution to bring down Jarvis. He had too many enemies, and that was the worst thing for any man to have. Beny didn't hesitate to bring Tameka into his employment. He needed a gutta bitch and someone to protect him from his enemies. Tameka as well wanted Jarvis, and she would have him, by all means.

"Benjamin . . . I will have him in no time now. Just promise to stop haunting me," Tameka prayed to Benjamin before she closed her eyes to get some much-needed rest. She was in one of Haitian Beny's opulent guest rooms in the mansion, feeling safer than ever since Jarvis had hurt and humiliated her at the club.

She was grateful to Big Dee, who carried her from the club and made sure that she was okay. She had one more person to see after she was scheduled to depart from Miami. She would meet that person tomorrow and then safely return to Georgia with four of Haitian Beny's Miami assassins.

Damn, I can't wait, she thought while closing her eyes.

* * *

Kwan and Jason were two cold-blooded killers from Jacksonville, who were both twenty-three years old and biological brothers. For hours now, they had been waiting for Jarvis to return to the studio. They were unable to introduce themselves to him earlier because of the company with Jarvis at the time. Older brother, Kwan, had to remind Jason to remain calm and not blow their cover. Jason was the hothead, while Kwan was the brains, whose advice and say-so had saved him and his brother from perilous situations before. Spin had agreed with Big Shawn to let the brothers turn Jarvis's day red. For some reason, ineffable to Big Shawn, he preferred to let his hounds handle this self-centered connect.

Darkness had fallen hours ago, and the brothers were still waiting to see Jarvis again.

"The door is opening," Jason said while grabbing his Mini-14 off the floor of the passenger side of the all-black Explorer.

Nobody's coming out yet, Kwan thought before he saw the gorgeous woman who had come to the studio with Jarvis earlier in the day.

They knew Jarvis was close, since she was just standing at the entrance of the door talking to someone inside the studio.

"That bitch is bad, bra . . ."

"Tell me about it!" Kwan retorted, admiring the gorgeous woman in the leopard minidress and black leather boots, with a succulent ass that bounced every time she took a step. Jason's dick was getting hard at the sight of her curvaceous body. But his lust turned into the taste for blood when he saw Jarvis and his entourage emerge from the studio.

"Showtime!" Kwan said, starting up the Explorer.

Jason quickly rolled down his window and positioned himself with the Mini-14 in his hands. As the Explorer swung around and the entourage was lined up with Jason's aim, a Hummer HZ limousine came from the opposite direction with its beams brightly illuminating the path of the Explorer creeping with its lights off. Everyone saw the gunman clear as day.

"Fuck!" Jason shouted as the bright lights blinded him.

Despite being unable to see the entourage, it was too late to turn back, so he squeezed the trigger and released a deadly fusillade.

Chat! Chat! Chat! Chat!

Boom! Boom! Boom! Boom!

"No! Aww!" Champagne screamed out in pain as a bullet pierced through her shoulder.

When she hit the ground, Jarvis landed on top of her and continued to squeeze his Glock .17 at the Explorer, as did his men, who returned fire at the moment the gunfire erupted.

Boom! Boom! Boom!

Jarvis's men ran the Explorer out of the studio's parking lot, causing the gunman to drop his weapon in the process, which was an indication that he was probably hit himself. As the taillights of the Explorer vanished into the darkness, Jarvis continued to lie on top of Champagne, who was crying and trembling from the shock of what had just happened . . . and from the pain in her shoulder.

"Jarvis . . . Jarvis! It hurts!" she said faintly.

"Hold on, baby! Hold on . . ."

"Antron . . . man! Get up, buddy!" Jarvis heard one of his men say.

But he wasn't looking at him. He was looking at Champagne, who was hit and fading away unconsciously from the pain and blood that she was losing.

"Damn, man! Call an ambulance. My baby hit!" Jarvis yelled out.

"Antron's dead, man!" was the last thing Champagne heard before darkness took her.

* * *

"Fuck!" Kwan screamed out as he accelerated the Explorer onto the interstate in search of the nearest hospital. Jason was hit from the deadly fusillade, taking two bullets in his chest and one in his neck. He was still holding on after three miles of traveling.

"Hang in there, little bro. We almost there . . ." Kwan yelled to his brother.

"Mmm . . . mmm . . . !" Jason moaned in pain while holding onto his bloody neck.

I can't believe this shit, Kwan thought.

"Damn it! That fucking HZ! Where the fuck did it come from?" Kwan cried out, with tears cascading down his face, praying and hoping that his little brother escaped the hands of death.

"We've come too far, little bro . . . too far!" Kwan cried out, wiping away his tears as they fell.

When he looked over at his brother, he saw Jason's eyes open and his chest and abdomen area inactive. Jason was soundless.

Jason!" Kwan screamed out to his brother, who gave no response. "We're almost there!" Kwan said, but Jason was already gone.

* * *

136

"Breaking news reporting . . . live from Channel 9 News . . . where a crime scene from late last night is still being investigated . . . and where the body of hip-hop rapper Antron King is still on scene behind me. There are still no leads to the suspects who left three individuals in critical condition, only one of whom is quickly recovering. Her name is Champagne Robinson, who suffered a shoulder injury from a single gunshot wound. Lucky for her, paramedics arrived in time to stop her tremendous blood loss. People . . . this is a sad thing to have happened, especially for the now deceased rapper Antron King. If there is anybody that can help bring justice to these people, please contact the Jonesboro Police Department at 200-6313-4074. Once again, reporting live . . . Channel 9 News at Money Green Records . . . still on the crime scene, this is Michelle Lucas," the beautiful black reporter concluded.

When Maurice looked over at Shaquana, she was in pain, something that was evident by her cascading tears. He put her in his warming arms, embracing her and letting her cry.

"It's okay, baby. She's okay!" Maurice said, for he knew why she was crying, despite her stubbornness to forgive. Shaquana still loved her friend enough to not lose her to death.

20

The entire town of Jonesboro and city of Atlanta were devastated at the loss of their local hip-hop rapper. Antron's fan base was like family. They were able to relate to his music, due to his old-school lyrics and generation.

His vigil was as crowded as one of his concerts. Many people came from all over the state to lay flowers and light candles on the bloodstained pavement where Antron took his last breath. The local authorities were locking up every black man who they deemed capable of committing the crime. After an interrogation, they were released if they didn't have any outstanding warrants. When Maurice and Shaquana pulled up to the studio to show their respect, they had to park a quarter mile away and walk on foot through the overcrowded streets.

After learning that Champagne was okay, Shaquana sent her flowers and a get-well card. The doctors were being meticulous and prohibited Champagne from having any visitors, since the shooters had not been caught—which meant that everyone was considered a suspect.

"Baby, this place is packed," Shaquana said to Maurice as they neared the spot where Antron's body had lain for hours.

"He's a celebrity, and many folks loved him, as you can see!" Maurice explained.

He could have been someone to date, if you—my king—would have never taken charge, Shaquana thought before quickly dismissing the direction in which her mind had attempted to take her.

She was aware that Antron had a thing for her, but her loyalty was with Donavon at the time.

And drinking too much liquor caused me to cheat on him by having a threesome with Maurice and Champagne. But, bitch, didn't you get your sober ass up the next morning and demand for some more of Maurice's dick? Shaquana's self-conscience asked her, causing her to laugh lightly.

"What's got you laughing, Ms. Giggles?" Maurice asked.

"Nothing. Just was thinking in the past of something Antron and Champagne did," she lied convincingly.

"Okay . . . I'll not bother to ask what it is," Maurice said.

"Please don't, because I promised them both that I wouldn't tell anyone," Shaquana said, again convincingly.

In her hands, she carried a bundle of fresh gardenia flowers that she laid on the tremendous pile of other varieties of flowers.

"May God be with you, Antron . . . and bring peace for your family," Shaquana said as tears fell from her eyes.

And thank you for dying for my friend, Shaquana thought as she hugged Maurice tightly.

"Thank you for being my rock, Maurice," she said as she wiped away her tears with the sleeves of her Polo sweater.

"I'ma always be your rock, baby. Believe that!" Maurice retorted as he placed his lips on hers and kissed her slowly and passionately.

* * *

Brenda was sitting in her living room watching the BET Music Awards when she saw headlights pull up in her driveway. *Who the hell is this?* she thought as she walked toward her front door and unlocked it. She opened the door and stood there. It took her a split second to realize that it was Maurice's conspicuous gray Range Rover sitting on 28-inch Forgiatos. She watched as both doors ascended in the air and Shaquana emerged from the driver's side in a fuck-me minidress and suede boots. Maurice got out of the passenger side and walked over to Shaquana's side. She then hit the button on her key chain, and the doors to the Range Rover descended.

"Well, I see ya'll stunting motherfuckers in the neighborhood today, huh?" Brenda asked, with her hands on her hips.

"Hello, Auntie Brenda!" Shaquana said wrapping her arm around her neck for a hug.

"Girl, what perfume is that? That shit smells good!"

"That shit does smell good, huh?" Shaquana said while digging in her Prada bag. When she found the bottle, she sprayed Brenda twice and said. "It's called Rogue . . . new RiRi (Rihanna)."

"It sure do smell good. Shit! Where's the bottle?" Brenda asked.

"You can have this one . . ."

"I hope you didn't think you were leaving here without handing it over," Brenda joked.

"How are you, Maurice?"

"Good, Brenda," Maurice retorted, giving her a hug.

* * *

The trio sat in the kitchen at the dining table and feasted on Brenda's delicious shepherd's pie while speaking about what everyone was desperately trying to piece together . . . Antron's death.

"I'm glad Champagne is okay. I tried calling her and was told that she was heavily sedated," Brenda explained to Shaquana and Maurice. "I even went by and saw Ms. Mae, and she did the most unordinary thing that you'd expect a grandmother to do."

"What did she do, Auntie?" Shaquana asked.

"She looked at me and said 'worse is to come to her' when I expressed my sympathy for Champagne," Brenda said, cocking her head back as if to say, "Really?"

Both Shaquana and Maurice looked stunned.

"Exactly! That's what was going through my head," Brenda said as she stood up and collected the empty plates.

As she walked into the kitchen, Maurice couldn't help but stare at her ghetto fabulous booty protruding from her gray sweatpants.

Damn . . . Brenda! he thought, lustfully grateful that Shaquana didn't catch him being mesmerized by her Auntie's succulent ass.

"Shaquana . . . bring them glasses unless ya'll want more wine," Brenda called out.

"I can't. I have to pee. That means you have to do it!" Shaquana said as she pointed at Maurice before she hastened to the bathroom upstairs.

"She just put your ass to work, mister!" Brenda joked to Maurice with a laugh.

"Don't worry. She'll pay for it later," Maurice said while collecting the glasses off the table to bring

141

to the sink where Brenda was washing the dirty dishes.

"I heard that right!" Brenda retorted.

"Sit them there!" she said while reaching over to open a cabinet, brushing her ass across Maurice's crotch area intentionally.

Wow! he thought as his dick instantly betrayed him.

"Excuse me . . . even though it's late!" Brenda giggled.

Maurice could tell that the wine was taking its toll and had Brenda feeling tipsy and horny.

"It's okay," he said with his dick throbbing.

When Brenda glanced at Maurice's jeans, she saw the bulge of his erection.

Oh my! she thought as her womanhood betrayed her and her nipples became hard and her plump mound between her legs got sultry.

Can't do this, girl! This is your niece's man, Brenda reminded herself.

"It's all good! So, what's up with Jerome . . . ?"

"Don't want to talk about him!" Brenda quickly fired back.

"Damn, that sounds like the dog house," Maurice said.

No, it sounds like he caught his bitch fucking another man, Brenda badly wanted to say, but instead she said, "No, just a small beef."

"So, what's up with Daquan?" Maurice asked.

"Nephew!" she sighed. "I'm still paying off the lawyer, though he wants an arm and a leg."

What you mean paying him off? Maurice thought.

"He thinks that $145,000 is a deal!" Brenda said.

When Brenda saw the look on Maurice's face, she became perplexed, because he looked like he couldn't understand the words coming from her mouth.

"Are you okay?" she asked while leaning back against her sink.

"Yeah! How much are you paying, if you don't mind me asking?" Maurice inquired.

I'm paying some good head and pussy, Brenda wished she could be frank. But it was not his business to know about her trading off her gorgeous body for her nephew to have a good defense attorney.

"I pay him what I can monthly from the money that Jerome gives me . . ."

"Seriously?" he asked of the lie she had just told him.

"Yes . . . serious, Maurice. It's h—"

"When was the last time you paid him?" Maurice asked the moment Shaquana walked back into the kitchen.

I just paid him some pussy and my relationship with Jerome, Brenda wanted to admit. But the look on Maurice's face demanded an answer. But he will not get the truth.

"I paid him $1,200 three days ago," Brenda said as she opened the refrigerator door and reached inside to retrieve her glass of wine.

"Damn, Auntie! Are we talking about Daquan's lawyer?" Shaquana asked.

"Yeah! The best in Atlanta, and an old school mate," Brenda said. "Classmate! Don't get it twisted."

"And a fuck nigga. I hope he ain't no friend of yours!" Maurice blurted out, shocking both Brenda and Shaquana with his sudden spitefulness toward Mr. Goodman.

"Are you okay, Maurice?" Brenda asked, feeling his forehead and checking him for a fever.

Shaquana stood puzzled, but she knew that something had suddenly angered her man.

"I'm okay, Brenda," Maurice retorted. "That nigga, Goodman, is playing you out of money that could be in your pockets, Brenda!"

"What am I missing here? My nephew is fighting a murder case, and no one is helping me pay no bills for his case. I had the house up for an option, until someone burned it down. I can't just let my nephew fall . . . !"

"Brenda . . . listen! Please!" Maurice said, grabbing her by her shoulders and staring into her eyes, which brought her ranting to a sudden halt.

Damn! Them some bedroom eyes, she thought.

Shaquana was completely confused as she stood beside Maurice.

"Mr. Goodman is a fuck nigga to accept any dime from you, and I will tell him myself. The only reason I won't find him and kill him myself is for Daquan's sake. I personally paid this man more than what he was asking for . . . Shit! Triple! And I told him not to disclose that I did so!"

Oh my God! Shaquana thought.

Now I understand. Goodman's playing me and fucking me freely, Brenda thought as the tears fell down her cheeks . . . for she was hurt and robbed of her relationship with Jerome because of deceitfulness.

She hugged Maurice and sobbed in his arms.

"Thank you, Maurice!" she cried out.

I'm going to kill him. I swear! she thought.

*   *   *

Tameka pulled up to the luxurious home in Liberty City outside of Miami, and smiled. Ol' girl has some nice taste, Tameka thought.

It was 9:00 a.m. and the area was quiet, with most neighbors already gone to work. It was a well-kept, wealthy neighborhood of well-appointed two-story homes and townhouses.

She's probably the only black woman in the neighborhood, Tameka thought as she grabbed her Louis Vuitton bag.

Tameka was dressed in a Polo suit that accentuated her delicate curves, and she wore Sergio Rossi pumps. Her skirt had a slit in the front that showed off her nice legs and partial thigh area. She put on her Marc Jacobs shades and let out a sigh before she emerged from the 2016 luxury-model Lincoln Town Car.

She took long strides as she walked toward the front door of the nice two-story home and admired the colorful flower bed outside the living room window.

So nice! Gardenias are my favorite, Tameka thought.

When she got to the front door, she sighed again before she knocked on the wooden door. She rapped five times and then immediately heard a familiar woman's voice call out from inside.

"I'm coming!"

Yeah, I know! Tameka thought.

A moment later, Tameka heard the locks on the door being disengaged as the door swung open to reveal a barefoot, heavy-set black woman in a sundress.

"Hello, stranger!" Tameka said.

"Get the hell out of here, woman! Damn! Tameka, girl . . . come in!" Marie said with a warming smile while embracing Tameka, the last person that she would expect to see on her front door step.

After Marie had received her share of Benjamin's money, she immediately packed her things and left Georgia, traveling further south until she landed in a beautiful Miami suburb. Marie had met an Italian businessman who traveled from Miami to New York as the CEO of a photography company for up-and-coming models, and she recently married him without a prenuptial agreement. After getting her money, Marie wanted to get as far away from the gang as she could, to live a comfortable life. Seeing Tameka again was as surprise to her, for she had no intentions of seeing anyone involved with Benjamin's death, ever again.

Inside the plush home, Marie settled Tameka in the nicely furnished living room that was the epitome of a black soul's taste in fashion. The lion, tiger, and elephant statutes on the antique tables epitomized a sister's traits.

"Anything to drink, Meka?" Marie asked.

"No, ma'am," Tameka answered, sitting on the black leather sofa with her caramel legs crossed while her Louis Vuitton rested on her lap.

"Damn, it's so good to see you. So how did you find me?" Marie asked with a smile as she sat in a leather Lazy Boy across from Tameka.

"I have my sources . . . plus, with money, no one can hide. Not even a dead man!" Tameka said, simultaneously removing her shades and placing them in her coat pocket.

The mention of a dead man made Marie feel eerie. She didn't know what it was, but she was unable to respond. She was speechless.

"It's okay, Marie. I know your conscience haunts you. Probably like me, huh?" Tameka said while looking into Marie's wide eyes.

What is she talking about? Marie thought. "I have no clue what you are talking . . ."

"Please! Let's not go there, bitch! I don't have no wires on me. Does Benjamin come to you like he comes to me?" Tameka asked.

This bitch is psycho! Marie though.

"Are you okay, Tameka? This don't seem like the same Meka," Marie said.

"Because it's not, Marie! I let a man turn me cold against a man who loved me better than him. And I understand everyone else's motive except for you. What made you turn against Benjamin, Marie? Huh?" Tameka said as she went through her Louis Vuitton and pulled out her Chrome .380 ACP with a pearl handle.

Oh my God! Marie thought, startled while looking at the gun in fear for her life.

"Tell me, Marie! What made you betray Benjamin? He sent me to ask you. Don't you think he deserves the truth?"

"Tameka, we are too good for this!" Marie said timorously.

"I know that already! That's why I'm here. Now tell me what I'm here to know!"

"What are you talking about, Tameka?"

"Bitch! Don't even play with me. The next thing coming out of your mouth better be what I asked of you," Tameka demanded, raising her voice sternly.

Oh my Lord! What is happening? Marie thought as perspiration instantly began to form on her upper lip and forehead.

"So, do he come and visit you?" Tameka said with her eyes closed.

Go now! Attack her now! Marie's self-conscience told her, but she was too afraid to move.

She estimated it would take her three long strides to get to Tameka. Being that she weighed over three hundred pounds, Tameka would be feeble under Marie's dead weight.

If only I could grab her and sit on her ass! Marie thought.

"Why? Why? Why, Marie, must we play these games?"

"He doesn't visit me, Meka . . . honestly!" Marie responded to her, causing her to erupt into hysterical laughter.

Now, Marie. Attack! Marie contemplated as she made a dash for Tameka.

Tameka's eyes flung open, and all Marie saw was the spark leaving the gun.

Boc! Boc! Boc! Boc! Boc!

Tameka squeezed the trigger repeatedly, hitting Marie multiple times in her face and chest. When Marie's body hit the plush white carpet, she stood over her and emptied the clip.

Boc! Boc! Boc! Boc!

Marie was lifeless after the first two slugs entered her forehead.

"Thanks from Benjamin, bitch! Don't worry . . . there's more to come behind you!" Tameka said before she turned and left the scene inconspicuously.

21

"Daquan Coleman Clark . . . you have a visit in booth ten," a male deputy's voice announced over the intercom.

"Damn, you lucky motherfucker! Because I was just about to pick all that shit up!" Daquan said to his new cellmate, Christopher Hall, who was a humble twenty-five-year-old, five foot nine black man from Atlanta. He usually stayed in the cell, reading Daquan's urban collection of Silk White.

The cellmates were on Daquan's bottom bunk, playing a card game called Rummy 500.

"Yeah, whatever! I'm 150 points away from smashing your ass," Christopher said, collecting all the cards and then shuffling them. "Yo! Don't forget. Be extremely careful," Christopher said to Daquan.

"I will. Don't worry," he responded, and then walked out of the cell to report to his visit.

When Daquan got into the chatty atmosphere, he surveyed the room to see who was in his vicinity. Jailhouse informants were among every inmate; in fact, six out of ten niggas were definitely reporting to the state attorney with information on another nigga's case, to free themselves. One of the main reasons Daquan stayed in his cell was to avoid running into an informant. Christopher was his fourth cellmate, and out of all of them, he was the only one Daquan trusted—because he was the only black cellmate that Daquan had ever had.

When he got to booth ten, Daquan saw Shaquana sitting behind the glass smiling, with the phone to her ear.

"What's up, Little Brother?" she said.

She seems so joyful . . . that's good! Daquan thought.

"What's good, big head?" he responded.

"Nigga, I know your tank-head ass ain't trying crack with your overcooked black ass!" Shaquana joked.

"You got that one. What's up, though?" he said, licking his dry lips.

"Shit crazy out here, Daquan. First it was Grandma and then Antron. It's crazy everywhere"

"I saw the news. How's 'Pagne?" Daquan asked.

"She's still in the hospital. The doctors have her on a wound-draining machine," Shaquana informed him.

"I hope she pulls through . . ."

"Daquan, she's okay. Though it was a close call."

"How's Auntie?"

"Devastated! But she tries to remain strong," Shaquana sighed.

"Daquan . . . Auntie recently just found out that your lawyer is cheating her out of money."

"How's that when he's paid for?" Daquan retorted.

"She's been paying him monthly, when he's been paid already . . ."

"Wait a minute, Shaquana! My lawyer told me that Auntie paid him $145,000. So what's the problem?" Daquan asked.

"Daquan," Shaquana said and then sighed, "Maurice paid your lawyer, unbeknownst to Auntie . . ."

"Maurice paid my lawyer?" Daquan asked, puzzled.

"Yes, he did, and he told your lawyer not to disclose that he paid the bill. Instead of telling Auntie to no longer give him money, your lawyer continues to take her money . . ."

Bitch-ass nigga! Daquan thought.

"Maurice wants to . . . you already know," Shaquana said, not wanting to talk reckless over the phone line, and being meticulous for her brother's sake.

I already know, Sis . . . fuck with a killer! Daquan thought. He had heard the rumors of Maurice's wrath and how he was the man in College Park who was extremely feared.

"So when will I finally meet Maurice?" Daquan asked Shaquana, who looked at her gold Rolex.

"In five more minutes. He's in the lobby and wants to finally meet you as well."

"Oh yeah?"

"Yeah. I also left you more money. Well, we both did," Shaquana said, smiling.

"That's cool, Sis, and I really appreciate everything," Daquan told her.

"Well, Little Brother, I'm a let Maurice come back here, and make sure you don't let your lawyer know that you're aware of his stunt. Auntie Brenda begged me to tell you that . . ."

"Why not confront him?" Daquan asked.

"Because like ya'll told me about being upset with Champagne . . ."

"It's not my place," both answered in unison.

"Okay!" Shaquana said as she stood up.

"I love you, Little Brother. Maintain . . . okay?"

"I will, Sis!" Daquan said. "And I love you too!"

Daquan then watched as his sister left.

Things couldn't play out better planned, he thought.

A minute had gone by before Daquan saw Maurice appear.

Damn! This nigga does look like Drake, Daquan thought.

When Maurice sat down at the booth, he immediately placed his closed fist to the glass and pounded Daquan's fist, showing him love.

"What's up, little soldier? I finally get a chance to meet ya. How's everything holding up for you in there?" Maurice asked Daquan.

"I'm maintaining, brah. You know any other young nigga would probably done folded and gave up, but not me. Feel me?" Daquan said while looking Maurice in his eyes.

"I feel you, brah. Continue to keep that spirit, and stay prayed up . . ."

"You know I be trying to find that divine connection, Maurice. But it's like it's so many directions to look in. So, I gave up trying to find him . . . I feel if there was a God, then why did this happen to me?" Daquan expressed.

"Listen, soldier . . . don't never question the man that can change bad to good . . . and good to bad. An ol' school once told me that when we question God, we doubt not only him but ourselves. All he expects us to do is ask when and if you still can't hear 'em . . . then just wait. For patience has always been a virtue," Maurice said to Daquan, who was seriously soaking up the advice and taking an instant liking to Maurice.

"Thanks, man. I really appreciate that food . . ."

"As long as you have food, you'll never starve, Daquan," Maurice retorted.

"That's true!" Daquan agreed. Now or never, Daquan thought.

"Yo, shawty. Can I ask you for a favor?" Daquan inquired.

"Anything, soldier," Maurice responded, all ears, willing to help his brother-in-law with whatever.

Daquan reached into the front pocket of the orange jumpsuit he was wearing and retrieved a small, folded piece of paper. Daquan quickly unfolded the paper that had a note written on it in bold letters, and pressed it to the glass so that Maurice would be able to read it. Maurice pulled out his iPhone and saved something to his planner data stored on his phone.

"How soon?" Maurice asked him.

"ASAP!" Daquan retorted.

There was a second of silence, during which time neither man spoke.

Please man, I need this to go through, Daquan thought.

"Do you trust it?" Maurice asked.

"If I didn't, I would have never brought it to you. I need help, brah . . ."

"And I got you. I'ma handle that like you've requested, brah, ASAP," Maurice told him.

"Thank you, brah. I o—"

"We family. I don't put family in debt. You don't owe me shit, remember that!" Maurice said.

"Booth 10 . . . thirty seconds until visit over," the male deputy's voice announced over the intercom.

"Do me a favor, Daquan?" Maurice asked.

"What's that?"

153

"Keep ya head up and circle small," Maurice said, placing his fist against the glass again.

"I got ya, shawty," Daquan shot back, with his fist to the glass.

Walking back to the cell block, Daquan was happy . . . for things turned out better than he'd planned. Now all he had to do was wait—something he had no problem doing.

* * *

"Okay, Champagne, you have another card and roses. Where am I going to put all these lovely flowers?" Champagne's doctor said.

She was a Latina in her mid-forties named Iliana Quintero, who had been taking care of Champagne as if she were her own child. Champagne was hooked up to a wound vacuum that provided sedation and drained the oozing.

"Where are we going to put this, young lady?"

"Who's it from?" Champagne asked as she took a swallow of her pecan ice cream.

"Ummm . . . let's see. It's from your friends Shaquana and Maurice."

"Can I see the card, please?" Champagne asked eagerly.

"Sure," Dr. Quintero responded as she placed the flowers next to the tremendous number of bouquets from classmates and neighbors. Champagne never thought that she had many people that actually cared for her. The only person she ever considered a friend was Shaquana. And she hated how her heart had become so cold, all for the love of a man who was cheating on his wife to fuck her. When Dr. Quintero handed her the card, she opened it and then read the caring words from her true friend and sister:

Dear Champagne,
Please forgive me for my stubbornness lately. I've really come to my senses and realized that I can't omit you from my life. Everyone makes mistakes and deserves to be forgiven. I cried my ass off because I didn't know how to deal with so much hurt all at once. I know my dad was a player before he became a damn player. So what, he was beating your back out. That's not my place to confront you. Your ass better be glad Renae ain't find out, because ol' girl would have taxed that ass (ROFL). For real, though, let's put this behind us, sister, and let's come together and get our shit together. Go back to school and study law. I want to find the ones responsible for my parents' deaths. What do you say? Get well and think about it.
Love always and forever,
Shaquana and Maurice

After reading the nice Hallmark card, Champagne looked at her doctor and smiled brightly.
"Dr. Quintero, thank you for everything," she said, on the verge of tears.
She was hurt, joyful, and seriously feeling regretful for taking her friends' mother from them. Champagne wanted to take her own life for the wrong that she'd caused. But she couldn't because she still would be hurting the people that loved her. Jarvis was going crazy worrying about her, and her grandmother was ill because she was stealing her government checks.

"You will be okay, Champagne, and it's my job to help," she heard Dr. Quintero say.

Suddenly, Champagne was tired again as she began to fade away from the sedation, but she could not remember ever taking the shot or pill. As she drifted away back to her dreamland, she thought about her friend, Shaquana.

She was happy that she had been forgiven, but there was still pain, because she was the one who had killed her friends' mom in cold blood—something that she could give neither of them back.

* * *

"Christopher Hall . . . pack your property and come to the officer's station. You're bonding out," the female deputy announced over the intercom.

It had just hit midnight and the moment that he'd been waiting for had arrived. Christopher jumped off the top bunk, excited and eager to taste his freedom. Daquan got out of his bunk and went to stand at the cell door, something he did out of habit.

"Damn, my nigga. This shit feels crazy. I can't believe how shit really be falling through for a nigga," Christopher said as he threw all his property into a pillow case.

"You just be on point out there, and keep your eyes on the road. It's niggas out there waiting to see you make your first mistake. Remember that!" Daquan warned.

"Listen to this young nigga dropping real wisdom. It's a reason why I fucks with you, shawty," Christopher said as he clapped hands with Daquan and embraced him. "Keep ya head on and ya game tight, my nigga. Everything's going to work out, so no need to sweat nothing. Real shit, shawty!" Christopher said to Daquan while looking in his eyes sincerely.

Click! Click!

The cell door's popping sound was an indication for Christopher to walk out of his cell.

"Love nigga . . . stay up!" Daquan said.

"You already know I'ma stay up, shawty!" Christopher answered back. "Alright, my nigga. Get some rest!" Christopher told him as he walked out of the cell, closing the door behind him.

Daquan watched as Christopher left the cell block, and smiled, for he knew that a real nigga had been released back to the streets.

"Now I got to make sure no police-ass nigga don't fall off in my cell," Daquan said quietly to himself.

He then crawled back into his bunk.

Before he closed his eyes, he said a silent prayer to himself and God: Dear Lord, let me prevail against my persecutors . . . and my enemies.

22

Tittyboo had just finished seeing his lawyer, Mrs. Brown, who was a gorgeous thirty-five-year-old, reputable black attorney. The news that she'd given had him devastated and wanting nothing to do with anyone that day, not even his cell mate, Lamar, and his new close friend, Joshah. The news made him feel skeptical about everyone.

How could a bitch I've been true to and taking care of turn against me? Tittyboo wanted to know.

He was dumbfounded as he read the same statement that Daquan had. It was hard for him to fathom her motive, because it was a woman who he thought loved him. Her missed visitations and refusal to accept his calls lately suddenly made sense. When he had inquired about her sudden lack of supporting him, she had obviously told him a lie when she stated that she had a new job.

She had a job alright: the bitch was working with the state, with a fabricated story, Tittyboo thought as he rubbed his face with his hands. His life was in the system's hands now, and they wanted him to fall for a murder he had nothing to do with. At this moment, he seriously hated Daquan because he still didn't see any effort from him in clearing his name in the murder.

I had nothing to do with this shit, and the nigga won't even be a man and free me from these chains! Tittyboo realized, feeling betrayed to all ends of the table.

"If it was me, I would free my nigga without him having to tell me shit." Tittyboo quietly said to himself.

He was confused and hurt and had no clue of where his case was headed. His lawyer explained to him the damage that Shay could do if she testified about her statement that she had given to the state attorney.

He sat back and thought hard about how he could get to Shay without incriminating himself. But he soon realized that there was no one he could trust like his best friend, Daquan. And from the looks of it, he was growing skeptical of him, too.

Tittyboo closed his eyes and prayed to God . . . the one he could trust, no doubt.

* * *

"Uhhh, baby! Damn, Maurice!" Shaquana purred as Maurice entered her deeply with slow rhythmic strokes. Maurice had Shaquana rolled into a cannon ball, giving her all of him like she'd begged for repeatedly.

"Harder, baby! Pleaseeee!" she begged, feeling herself on the edge of another powerful orgasm.

Maurice did as she told him, fluctuating his pace and thrusting. Their bodies were covered in sweat, ironically, with Keith Sweat emanating from their surround sound.

"This what you want, huh?" he inquired.

"Yes! Yes! Uhh, shit!" Shaquana screamed out ecstatically.

"Damn! I love you, girl!" Maurice called out as he felt himself coming to his load. Shaquana felt him tensing up and began working her pussy muscles and cumming to her creamy load.

"Ugghh!" she yelled.

"Arrghhh!" Maurice groaned out as he released his load inside her. "Damn, baby!" he said breathlessly.

"I love you, daddy!" Shaquana said as she pecked him on his lips and then kissed him passionately as he stayed plunged inside her womb, draining his love tool.

"I love you too, baby!" he retorted as he then pulled out of her while embracing her from the back. He was exhausted and only wanted to hold his lady until dawn.

He had a big day ahead of him. He was ready to make things happen for him and his circle in College Park. At noon he would be meeting his cocaine connect to purchase one hundred kilos, and then he would immediately hit off his plungs (clientele) with the product. Much as he was tired of competing against niggas in the dope game, he refused to let Haitian Beny regulate his turf.

The coward-ass niggas Romel and Beny are hiding like bitches, but I have something that'll make both of them niggas show their faces, Maurice thought.

"What are you thinking about?" Shaquana asked while turning around to look Maurice straight in his eyes.

"How do you know I'm thinking of something? I could just be lying here with a blank mind," Maurice inquired.

"True, but not even a peaceful mind is clear of thought," she said sententiously.

"I love your prudence, baby. It's so much truth in every word you've just said," Maurice said. "But I'm just thinking about some shit you don't even need to have on your mind," he said honestly.

"Okay . . . if there's anything that you feel I need to know, baby, then I'm here," Shaquana retorted. She wasn't the type of woman to pressure her man about anything, and Maurice loved that about her. Most of all, her mind didn't go into negative speculation, like if he was leaving her for the next bitch involved with him.

She is most definitely one of a kind, Maurice realized.

Shaquana had been putting some serious thought into returning back to school and seeking a career in law. She felt that there wasn't a more suitable time to speak on it with him than now, so she asked, "Baby, I'm thinking about going back to school. I can't linger out here without an education. I want to know how you feel about that?"

Maurice looked at Shaquana for a split second and then propped up on his elbows. She climbed on top of him, straddling him while rubbing her hands on his nicely shaped eight-pack abs.

"I think it's a smart move now rather than waiting until you're up in age. You may miss this graduation, but pulling off another year wouldn't hurt you. Then you could really seek your dream and become a cosmetologist," Maurice said.

"Baby, I don't want to be a cosmetologist no more!" Shaquana retorted.

Damn! A change of plans! Maurice thought. "So, what's your new interest?" he asked.

Here we go, Shaquana thought as she sighed deeply before speaking. "I want to study law, baby!"

Shaquana said while pulling damp hair out of her eyes.

Law huh? Maurice thought. "What part of law are you interested in?" he asked.

"I don't know. I want to find the bitches who killed my parents . . ."

What about the ones who were supposed to kill your daddy . . . like me? he thought.

"I feel that I owe my parents that much, baby," Shaquana exclaimed.

"Baby! To do that, you'll have to go looking for the bad guys, and that's . . ."

"I know . . . police work. Then maybe that's what I need to get into, like a detective," Shaquana said, sensing the change in Maurice's demeanor.

Hell no! That's not going to happen! Maurice thought. "So, you ready to become a police officer just to find the killers of your parents'?" Maurice asked.

"Is it a problem, baby?" she asked, crossing her arms.

"Hell yeah it's a problem. Are you forgetting who your nigga is? Are you ready to be around the motherfuckers who want me in prison, huh?" Maurice said, raising his voice.

No he didn't just go there! Shaquana thought. "Is that what you're concerned about, Maurice? Do it look like I want my man fucking incarcerated? How dare you!" she screamed, attempting to run away from him as he quickly grabbed her arm.

"Sorry, baby. I'm sorry. Just listen to me, okay. Woman . . . I love you, and I've never loved a woman in my life the way I love you, baby. I'm not going to sit here and discourage you from becoming what you want to. It's just . . . the life I live, baby, would, soon as it starts, begin to conflict with your career . . . and shit will fall apart. I just know . . . !'"

So, we're not as strong as I thought, she reflected. "Well, get out of the streets. You have money to wash and come out a winner," Shaquana said effusively while patting her chest.

Maurice looked at Shaquana and saw the love that she had for him written on her face. She wanted him to leave the streets alone and become a different statistic than failure. But Maurice wasn't ready to give up the game that made him the man he was today. His father was killed in front of him when he was eight years old, which is what turned him cold and an addict to murder. Shortly after that, his mother was raped and killed, leaving him alone with no other siblings and cousins other than D-Rock. It was the streets that raised Maurice, and it was all he knew.

"Baby . . . listen. I can't leave the streets as of now. I'm sorry if them aren't words that you want to hear from me. But I can't lie to you. I'ma always keep it real, because I love you. If this can help you change your mind, I hope so, but I've been searching for your parents' killers every day, Shaquana. And I know that soon I will stumble across . . ."

"Don't use my parents' murder as an excuse, Maurice! I will find them myself. You've already told me that you're not leaving the streets. Maurice . . . the streets only promised two things . . . both of which are tragedies: death and incarceration," Shaquana told him as she got up off of him.

This time Maurice let her go without protesting.

When she walked to the shower and closed the door, Maurice sighed and then lay back against the mirrored headboard.

What Shaquana had said was true, but Maurice was naive and not ready to let the street life go.

Damn it! he thought, stressed and rubbing his temples.

*   *   *

When Mr. Goodman pulled up to the Hilton Hotel in his S-Class Benz, he applied another touch of his Jordan cologne. "Now let's get this party started!" Goodman said as he stepped out of the pearl-white Benz.

He had told his wife, Tabatha, that he would be working late in the office that night so that she wouldn't bother staying up with dinner for him.

As he strutted toward the entrance of the luxurious hotel, he saw a woman who looked so much like his wife, Tabatha, except she was a little too curvy around the hips.

Tabatha will never have delicate hips like these, Goodman thought as he watched the woman and her date walk away from the hotel.

Inside the lobby, Mr. Goodman walked straight to the elevator and took it up to the tenth floor. Stepping off, he met eyes with a beautiful brunette dressed in a sexy blue minidress that accentuated her delicate curves.

"Hello, gorgeous," he said to the lady.

"Hi, sir," she retorted, blushing.

She waved at him as the doors closed, and he almost hopped on the second elevator to catch up with her, but he instead continued on to his destination.

He walked down the hallway until he stood in front of hotel suite 202.

"Here we go!" he said as he rapped on the door five times.

When the door swung open, Goodman's dick instantly became erect while staring at the gorgeous sister that looked so much like Toni Braxton. She stood there in sexy black satin lingerie with handcuffs and a whip in her hands.

"So what, you just going to stand there . . . or come take this pussy like a man?" Brenda asked him, an understatement that Goodman missed.

"You ready for this?" Goodman said as he went to reach out and grab Brenda.

However, she backed up further into the suite and swayed her index finger from side to side.

"No, mister! Please turn around and close the door, and then put your hands behind your back . . . for you are under arrest for being pussy whipped!" Brenda teased.

"Oh yeah!" Goodman responded as he closed the door and followed her orders.

* * *

Brenda straddled Goodman, who was handcuffed by his wrists and ankles to the canopy bed. She began to have her way with him. She sucked his dick and performed some extraordinary foreplay on him that he was unable to resist. She brought out her toys and played with Goodman's asshole with dildos and anal beads. She was turning him out, all for the hidden camera to record.

He had fucked up her relationship with Jerome, the only man she had given her heart to since Earl's father was killed. Jerome hadn't called her, and she didn't know how to call him. The look in Jerome's eyes the day he caught Brenda having sex with Goodman was the epitome of real unforgiven pain.

Exhausted and confused, Goodman let Brenda slowly ride his dick. When he felt himself coming to another load, she must've sensed it too, because she climbed off of him and began stroking his enormous love tool while licking his asshole.

"You like this shit, huh?" she asked.

"Uhh! Shit!" Goodman purred.

For over an hour, she continued to give Goodman more than he could handle . . . or ever expect.

"Do you like this shit? Speak up, Daniel. I can't hear you . . . !"

"Damn. I love it when you call me by my first name!" Goodman yelled out. "Arrgghh! Shit!" he groaned, releasing his load for the fourth time.

"Shit!" he exhaled tensely.

"Okay, now one more thing before we cut the camera!"

Camera! Goodman thought when Brenda mentioned the word. "What you mean camera, girl?" Goodman asked, laughing as if it were a joke.

"Come on now, Daniel. This shit too good not to put on display," she said to him, getting off of the bed. She then pointed at her iPhone that was attached to the wall at a downward angle to catch a full view of the bed.

"Bitch! What are you doing?" Goodman screamed hysterically. I can't believe this bitch! he thought to himself.

"Come on, Daniel Goodman. You're fucking business up now. Why are you overreacting?"

"Overreacting! Bitch, what you are recording me for, huh?"

"Wait! I'll be back," Brenda told him as she stormed off to the bathroom.

"Brenda, come here. I'm serious. Erase that shit!" Goodman continued to scream while looking up at the iPhone camera.

When Brenda returned, she was fully dressed in her black H&M off-the-shoulder dress and Bebe heels.

"Brenda! What's going on? Why are you tripping?" Goodman asked her, calming his voice down.

"Listen here, you gay motherfucker! And don't say you're not because no man takes a dildo in his ass. I don't care how much power pussy have . . . !"

"Bitch . . . !"

"Call me another one, and Tabatha will be the first motherfucker to see how much of a homo you are . . . then your fucking kids will see it with the world!" Brenda threatened as she removed her heels and stood on top of the dresser to remove the iPhone.

"Why is this occurring? Where did this sudden change come from? This is business, remember?" Goodman exclaimed as Brenda climbed back down from the dresser and slipped back into her heels.

"So this is business, right?" Brenda asked while fast-forwarding their sex tape to the part when she was fucking Goodman with the dildo and beads.

"Look how your asshole looks!" Brenda said as she walked up to him and showed him the footage that would destroy his career and relationship with a bitch who he had married without a prenuptial agreement. A divorce would take him out of the game and risk all that he'd worked hard for.

"Brenda, why did you do this?" he asked sternly.

"Goodman. A fellow . . . excuse me . . . a nice fellow came to your office one day and paid you a lump of money to represent my nephew . . ."

Damn! he thought, understanding everything now.

"From my understanding, he wired you $400,000 and wanted it to remain . . . what's the word again," she said, snapping her fingers, trying to recall the word. "Anonymous!" she blurted out. "Yeah, he wanted to remain anonymous, but he paid the entire bill. And tell me . . . what did you do?" Brenda asked while looking at Goodman, who was at a loss for words.

"I'm sorry, Brenda."

"I know you are, Daniel. For years we've known each other for good time's sake. We were classmates. I came to you with my body to pay for my nephew to have a good lawyer. And you played me, Goodman. A real man would have kept it real, but you took advantage and caused me to lose a good man. So now I'ma cause you havoc if you do not get my nephew home. Now from here on out, until my nephew is a free man, let's keep this strictly business. You do what you have to do, and I promise you this footage will never be seen," Brenda explained, waving her iPhone in the air.

"Have a nice night, Goodman!" Brenda said, leaving the suite with all her toys in her Prada bag.

"Untie me, Brenda! Come on!" he screamed as he heard the door slam shut.

"Fuck!" he exclaimed as he began to wait for the housekeeper to arrive in the morning and find him.

168

23

When he pulled up to the address written on the white piece of paper that he had in his hand, he double-checked and saw that he was indeed at the right place.

He sighed and then looked around to survey his surroundings, and he saw nothing amiss. He pressed the button on his digital G-Shock watch, and the green light illuminated for a split second revealing 3:00 a.m.

I could have waited for another hour, but it would be useless, for time these days is of the essence, he thought.

He reached under the seat and retrieved his silencer P89.

"My baby," he said, tucking the P89 in his waistband to his black jeans.

From the passenger side seat, he grabbed a pair of black leather gloves and slid them on. He flexed his hands to slide into them fully and then adjusted his black skully.

"Showtime!" he said as he inconspicuously emerged from his stolen Audi.

He quickly blended in with the darkness and listened to the distant dogs barking. It was drizzling and promising another rain shower. When he stood in front of apartment 301, he knelt down and put his hand under the foot ledge until he felt what he was searching for.

"Got it!" he mumbled out loud as he peeled the spare key from the base of the ledge before standing back up.

He immediately placed the key into the door to unlock it.

Let's go! he thought as he turned the knob and entered the cold apartment.

"Uhh . . . ummmm! Yes! Damn, Harry!" a woman moaned out from one of the bedrooms.

He pulled out his P89 and quietly followed the moans and sounds of the two bodies clashing at every penetrating thrust, and the squeaky bed and headboard rattling.

"Damn! This dick is good, Harry!" she purred out to her lover.

He walked by the first bedroom and then turned back to walk inside. There he came across two unique bunk beds with sleeping children. Altogether, there were four kids—three boys and one very young girl—all between the ages of ten months and five years. He could kill them all, but they were sleeping. To kill them would be overdoing what he was there to do. But he couldn't say the same if they were to suddenly awake. To avoid doing that, he moved on and walked out of the room.

"Uhhh, shit!" she moaned out as she came to her orgasm.

"That's right, baby! Arrgghh!" Harry said exploding inside the woman's womb.

When he came into the doorway, the room was illuminated by the glowing TV that was on mute. Harry was still stroking his load onto the woman's back.

Perfect! he thought as he aimed at the back of Harry's head and then squeezed the trigger twice, sending brain matter onto the walls of the room and onto Shay's back, imbuing the sheets and walls with blood.

"What the fuck!" Shay exclaimed when she felt the spray of blood splatter onto her back. She heard the muffled sounds that the silencer P89 made, but she was too ingenuous to match the distinctive sound to a pistol.

When she saw Harry fall down next to her, she saw death staring back at her. But that only lasted a second, because Christopher silenced her with two slugs to her face.

"Bitch! That's why ya dead now. All that damn screaming!" he said as he walked up on her and pulled the trigger repeatedly.

When he was done, Christopher quickly left the apartment inconspicuously while a heavy downpour of rain fell on Jonesboro, Georgia.

* * *

"Get the fuck out of here!" Detective Barns exclaimed as he got off the phone with his chief of police, who had just delivered the most devastating news to him about Shay's murder.

"Is everything alright, baby?" his wife, Chythia, asked while pouring hot Maxwell House coffee into his twenty-year-old mug.

"No!" he said as he sighed. "Somebody just killed our star witness in Daquan Clark's case . . ." And the good piece of pussy I had on the side, he thought.

"Oh my God! What happened?" Chythia exclaimed, sitting down at the table with her husband.

JACOB SPEARS ~ TRAYVON JACKSON

She had a gorgeous resemblance to Coco, Ice-T's wife, as well as her voluptuous body. She was still carrying the beauty from her stripping days, when her name was Beth.

"Chief says someone broke into the apartment, despite no signs of forced entry, and killed her and a lover, possibly the ten-month-old's father," Detective Barns said to Chythia.

Chythia was a detective as well, but she worked in the Atlanta district for the Atlanta Police Department. She was also working herself toward a promotion to become a lieutenant in the Major Crimes Department.

"So, I'm guessing the chief wants you to take lead on the case?" she inquired, taking a sip of her steaming cup of coffee.

"Yeah. That's exactly what he wants!" Barns said to her with a sigh.

He couldn't believe that his key witness had been killed. She was a critical witness, who would have convinced the jury to convict Tittyboo and Daquan. But now he was back to square one.

Damn it! he thought.

"Baby! I'll see you later. I have to get over to the crime scene," Barns said as he stood up and slid into his coat that was hanging on the back of this chair. He then walked over to his wife and embraced her while kissing her passionately and rubbing on her succulent ass.

"Ummm!" she moaned as their tongues fought with each other.

"See you tonight, okay?" he said.

"Okay. I love you . . ."

"I love you too," he retorted as he kissed his wife one more time before leaving the house.

172

* * *

When Detective Barns arrived at the crime scene, he crossed behind the yellow crime tape and met up with his partner, Detective Cunniham, who briefed him on the status of the investigation. Crime scene investigators were all over the two-bedroom apartment doing their jobs perfectly as experts trying to find evidence to bring the suspect down.

"So, what's your insight?" Barns asked his partner.

"I thought that I'd leave that open for you to answer. Thus far, we've found nothing but two dead bodies and four kids . . ."

"And no witnesses!" both partners said in unison.

Damn it! he thought as he walked past his partner and into the room where Shay and her lover's body lay in the bloodstained bed.

This is not happening to me. Where is the killer? he asked himself.

"Cunniham!" he called.

"Yes!" Detective Cunniham answered, standing behind Barns.

"This was a hit either by Daquan or Tittyboo. Why wouldn't their motive be logical?" he asked her.

When Detective Cunniham looked over at her partner, she saw the bulldog in his eyes. She knew that when he had that look on his face, he was onto something.

"I think you're right, Barns . . . but how do we prove it?" she said to him.

"If there's a will . . . then there's a way!" he responded.

* * *

When Tittyboo heard inmates shouting out that a crime scene was occurring in his hood, he laid his book down on the bunk and walked out into the wing's dayroom. At the same time, he looked down from the top tier at the news report on the television to see a black reporter named Michelle Lucas standing behind the crime scene.

Damn! That's my . . . !

"Yo, Titty . . . that's your shit!" one of the niggas from Tittyboo's hood named J-Rock screamed out.

The look on Tittyboo's face showed that he was in shock and confused at the discovery of the double murder. The news reporter went on to explain that Shay Graham and her lover, Harry Wilson, were murdered. Despite his heart being broken by the revelation, Tittyboo was grateful and thanked God for answering his prayers.

It had to be God, because I prayed long and hard for that ho to go missing, Tittyboo thought as he walked back into the cell and resumed reading his Silk White novel titled The Teflon Queen.

"Well, that's how it is!" Tittyboo said and then sighed with tremendous relief, for Shay testifying about a fabricated statement against him and Daquan was no longer his worry.

*   *   *

When Daquan saw the breaking news in his hood, he wasn't nearly as surprised. He was elated, and he realized at that moment just how powerful a Clark was. He knew that he could trust Christopher to get the job done, that's why he had Maurice bond Christopher out. Christopher was a straight killer, who trusted Daquan with some things that killers just didn't talk about. He had been arrested on charges of possession of a firearm by a convicted felon. Being that Christopher wasn't from Jonesboro, the judge enhanced his bond to $200,000 . . . money that no one is his own family had or could afford. As their days went on, he and Daquan bonded and Daquan had foreseen the potential in Christopher to get rid of the state's witness: Shay.

Now it's time for plan B to take off. In no time, all these crackers will be in fear of anyone with the last name of Clark, Daquan thought as he sat on his bed and read Shay's fabricated statement for the umpteenth time. No more worries!

* * *

Maurice was no fool and had easily put two and two together after seeing the news. Shaquana lay in his arms after making love and had no clue about the man responsible for the double murder, nor was she aware that Shay was a deadly weapon against her brother's defense.

A lot of shit is meant to be left unsaid because the right time isn't always an opportunity, Maurice thought as he closed his eyes. So that was the star snitch, and Christopher was the terminator, he thought retrospectively of Daquan's note that he had shown Maurice at visitation.

Christopher was now a potential teammate who Maurice was interested in, and he had every intention of using him as a hit man himself.

When Shaquana had fallen asleep—something she did every time Maurice fucked her good, long, and hard—he slid out of bed and put on a pair of

Jordan shorts. He then grabbed his iPhone off the oak nightstand and walked into the living room.

As he sat down on the black leather sofa, he sighed and then called a stored phone number. The phone rang twice before the caller picked up.

"Hello!" Christopher answered.

"Yo! You already know who this is . . ."

"Yeah, what's good, shawty?" Christopher said.

"You just landed yourself a job that you can't refuse," Maurice told him.

"Oh, yeah? What makes you figure that, shawty?" Christopher wanted to know.

"Because it's too many numbers involved, shawty!" Maurice retorted.

"I kept my word. Daquan . . . that's my boy . . . and he helped me out. So I have no problem fucking with you for the numbers," Christopher said, accepting Maurice's offer.

"We'll call you C-Murder," Maurice said to him.

"What? That comes with the job?" Christopher asked.

"Naw. That comes with the team, shawty!" Maurice retorted and then hung up.

C-Murder will definitely help set these niggas straight, Maurice thought as he crawled back in bed with Shaquana.

24

Champagne was happy to be home and able to be catered to by Jarvis. Despite her shoulder injury, Jarvis was able to make love to her gently and erase the pain that lingered by causing her electrifying orgasms that had been on hold two long weeks. Jarvis had just stepped out after making love to her and assisting her in a hot, steaming shower, where they made love again. Now she was lying in their comfortable canopy bed chatting on the phone with Shaquana, who was surprised at the revelation of Champagne and Jarvis's relationship.

"Damn, bitch! I knew that your pussy got wet from looking at that nigga . . . !" Shaquana teased.

"Whatever, Shaquana! Like I said . . . that shit happened by chance," she told her.

Champagne told Shaquana about the whole incident that had happened at the club when Jarvis pulled her from the stage and then stomped her boss to sleep.

"Yeah, bitch! You knew what you were doing when you started working there, bitch. A dog ain't a dog if he bypasses any meat!" Shaquana said as she burst into laughter.

This girl is still a damn fool! Champagne thought, realizing how much she had missed her friend.

Despite being surprised by Champagne's relationship, Shaquana had no intentions of exposing her ill feelings toward Jarvis and her speculation on him knowing something about the ones who were responsible for her father's and mother's deaths. That, she would keep to herself, and she would pursue the killers herself, even if it took her twenty years to accomplish. What she did want to talk to Champagne about was her decision to return to school . . . and then law school.

"Champagne, what do you think about going back to school?"

The line went silent for a few seconds before Champagne spoke up. Shaquana could picture the perplexed expression on her friend's face.

"School? I never thought about that shit! I stopped going because I ain't want to deal with the many questions about our break-up . . ." And I was scared to let people know that I was pregnant from your dad, even though I lost the baby, Champagne contemplated.

"Listen, 'Pagne. It's not too late to graduate. Shit, we . . ."

"Missed our damn year, Shaquana!" Champagne retorted, cutting off Shaquana.

Don't I know that! Shaquana thought. "Champagne, we could still make next year. Shit! It's better than falling years behind without an education. You don't want to be out here like most of these hos with bills and dumb on how to pay them. And neither Jarvis nor Maurice ain't promise to always be around. Champagne . . . we could do something about it! Better today than later."

What she is saying is so true, but what the fuck do I want to do after? Be back in the same position as a hustler woman? I don't know! Champagne thought.

"Shaquana, just let me think about it. But until then, don't wait on me. Go sign back up and . . ." This isn't Champagne! Hell no! She would have agreed in a heartbeat, Shaquana thought.

Although it upset her to see her friend being indecisive for the first time, she was never one to force anything on anyone. But she still wanted to know what Champagne would think about her wanting to then go to law school.

"Champagne, you know how I wanted to become a cosmetologist?" Shaquana asked.

"Yes . . . and you still c—"

"I don't want to be that no more . . ."

"What! Now you want to be a stripper too? Damn! I should have never told your ass that!" Champagne exclaimed in jest.

"Shut up, crazy. The only mother fucker I'm stripping for is Maurice!" Shaquana said, meaning every word of what she had just said.

"So what's new then? Break me off!" Champagne said, ready to be enlightened to her friend's new interest.

"Champagne, I want to find the ones responsible for killing my parents, so I'm going to go to law school to become a detective. What do you think?" she asked.

There was silence again for a jiffy that both women wished had never occurred.

I killed your mom, but I'm sorry! Champagne thought before she broke down. Unable to respond, she hung up the phone on Shaquana before she could discover her emotional breakdown as she cried hysterically and regretted the terrible thing she had done to her friend's mother. "Why! Why! Why!"

Champagne sobbed, never hearing the intruder that was in the home she shared with Jarvis.

* * *

"What the hell, Champagne?" Shaquana yelled into the phone after hearing the line go dead. Her damn phone must've went dead or something, Shaquana thought.

To make sure, Shaquana dialed Champagne's number again, just to hear the call go directly to voice mail.

"Yeah! Her phone went dead," she said as she then walked into her and Maurice's bedroom, where she stripped out of her clothes and hopped into a hot bubble bath. She wanted to smell and taste delicious to Maurice that night when he got home.

"I love that man to death! Lord, please protect us and not let my decisions come between real love, Lord!" Shaquana prayed out loud while soaking in her strawberry bubble bath.

* * *

Getting into their home was an easy task because she had an extra key herself. She knew that Jarvis wasn't in the house, because she'd watched him leave an hour earlier. And being that it was 12:00 a.m., she knew that he was heading over to the club. As she crept toward the master bedroom, she could hear Champagne's cries. Then she heard her cry out loud.

"Why did I have to kill her? She was my friend!"

Wow! she thought. I wonder what skeletons this bitch has in her closet?

A hurt dog would always scream when it was hurt.

"Please, God, forgive me!" Champagne said, sniveling.

Forgive me for what? For what do you need to be forgiven? the intruder so desperately wanted to know as she stood outside Champagne's door and listened to her vent more.

"Lord! I killed this girl's mother out of love, and it was wrong. Please, Lord!" she said again, sniveling.

Champagne was in so much pain mentally that she felt no pain from her injury at all.

So, this bitch kills her friend's mother just to be with Benjamin! the intruder thought to herself, drawing the conclusion from Champagne's confession.

Hearing no more confessions, the intruder appeared in the doorway of the bedroom and saw Champagne lying on the bed in a fetal position, ceasing her crying. Her back was toward the intruder as she cried. The intruder's hands held a two-foot-long piece of rope, wrapped around her knuckles. As the intruder crept forward, Champagne began to vent again.

"How could I be so damn selfish? Renae was my friend, and I was wrong to be fucking her husband."

You just now figure that out? The intruder thought as she neared Champagne, closing the gap, almost to her.

"Lord, I really need you to . . ."

Before she could finish her sentence, the intruder's hands swiftly wrapped her neck with the rope and began to throttle her.

"Nooo!" Champagne managed to squeeze out. But when she tried to lift her arm, a sharp pain erupted from her shoulder, causing her to become more defenseless. Before she knew it, Champagne's world turned completely black, and she passed out—unconscious.

"Sorry, baby girl, but this shit is really personal!" the intruder said as she let up on the pressure around Champagne's neck. She didn't want to throttle her to death, for she had further plans for Champagne. Then she would kill her.

*   *   *

Romel was sitting on the leather sofa in his suite, smoking on a hefty dro blunt while exhaling the smoke in sections of clouds, when his phone rang.

Grabbing his iPhone off his lap, he saw that it was Haitian Beny.

"'Bout time this nigga called me," Romel said, for he'd been waiting to hear from Beny to take credit for Antron's murder.

Though he wasn't responsible, he felt like Haitian Beny would never know.

He wanted Antron dead, and that's all that matters, Romel thought.

"Hello!" Romel answered, exhaling smoke from his mouth.

"What's good, my man? I see you know how to hit 'em up real good," Beny said in Creole.

"Yeah, I had to send a couple niggas to handle that. We still got work to do, as you can see," Romel retorted.

"Yeah, yeah, yeah! I feel yo. Good job, by the way . . ."

"Business is always good," Romel retorted.

"Okay, ummm . . . I need to run something by your way to have you up on ten toes," Haitian Beny said.

"Go ahead!" Romel insisted.

"Jarvis will be an easier task than I thought, but I still need you. Do you know Shaquana Clark?" Beny asked.

Romel thought for a second, trying to pinpoint the name that sounded so familiar to him, but he couldn't recall from where and who she was.

"That name sounds familiar," Romel said as he heard a knock at his door.

He looked at his gold Rolex and saw it was 1:30 a.m.

That has to be Markeina, he thought as he walked over to open up the door while still conversing with Beny on the phone.

"It sounds familiar because of her dad who just got killed. The CEO of —"

"Money Green Records!" Romel said, finishing the sentence while opening up the front door.

Like he had expected, it was Markeina.

"Hi!" she whispered while waving her hand and walking inside. When she walked past Romel, she stopped and leaned toward him, planting a kiss on his cheek.

"Yeah, umm . . . I remember now. What's up with that?" Romel asked Haitian Beny in Creole, which Markeina understood well, unbeknownst to him.

"I need her and her family wiped out!"

"Don't she rock with Chad's girl, Champagne?" Romel asked.

"Yeah, and Shaquana fucks with our boy Maurice . . . and Champagne is now with our boy Jarvis . . ."

"Get the fuck outta here! So, all a nigga got to do is grab her ass?" Romel inquired.

"You well know how the game goes, son. If we can't get you, then that bitch is up for grabs, just like in the game of chess!" Haitian Beny said. "So don't worry about Jarvis. We'll talk later about him. Just bring me Shaquana . . . alive!" Beny concluded as he hung up the phone.

Ten-four, nigga, Romel thought.

He heard pots being rummaged through, and caught up with Markeina in the kitchen. When he saw her, he walked up behind her, wrapped his arms around her, and then kissed her on the nape of her neck.

"Damn, that feels good . . . but not . . . ," she started, standing in front of the stove.

She could feel Romel's bulging erection on her ass as she reached around to grab ahold of it.

Her miniskirt and heels had him ready to take the pussy that he still hadn't gotten a chance to dive into.

Damn! He's a girth king! Markeina thought.

And this bitch still want to play these teasing games, Romel thought.

"Calm down, baby! Be nice!" Markeina said, causing Romel to erupt into laughter.

"Woman! You a trip!" he exclaimed as he walked over to the minibar and sat down on one of the stools. He watched Markeina prepare a dinner, and lustfully imagined how it would be to make her his wife. Every street nigga needs a wife to come home to at the end of the day, he thought. "Just tell me I'm not too far from being the one to satisfy you," Romel blurted out to Markeina.

"Boy, what are you talking about?" Markeina said, with a smirk on her face.

"I'm talking about us . . . being together, baby!" Romel answered.

"We are together, Romel. We're just not rushing into bed. Like I told you, I'm different from them hos that are out there."

I know that. That's what turns me the fuck on more, he thought. "I know, baby . . . and like I said, I'm still waiting," Romel began before he left to hop in the shower. "I'ma take a shower. I'll be out in a few."

Markeina just watched him walk away, with a smile on her face. Nigga, please . . . I know game when I see it, she thought. But he did get this pussy wet just a few minutes ago. I just can't do it. He'll never be for me; maybe in another life, Markeina finally told herself, something that she always did when she was in one of her confounded moments.

In the hot, steaming shower, Romel stroked his erect manhood and envisioned that he was fucking Markeina from the back while she stood at the stove. The smell of onions lingered redolently in the air and put reality to his imagination.

"Damn it! Stop teasing me and give daddy that pussy!" Romel whispered out, rapidly masturbating.

Damn! he thought lustfully when he saw the sex face that Markeina had in his mind. Her mouth was wide open, unable to utter a moan, as he rammed his dick into her wet pussy.

"That's right, baby! Take this dick. Arrgghh!" Romel moaned as he came to an electrifying orgasm, shooting his semen down toward the drain. "Damn it, girl!" he exclaimed to himself. "When I do get that pussy, your ass is in trouble!"

25

"Yo, Big Dee! Don't forget to take the money in the safe over to the bank, shawty . . ."

"I got you, shawty!" Big Dee retorted to Jarvis over the phone.

After he had hung up, Big Dee prepared to close down the club. All the strippers were gone except for Coco, who had immediately replaced Tameka as the person in charge, after being voted in by the other girls. Coco was also Big Dee's sidekick, and she had him wrapped around her fingers. Her five four pecan, Coke-bottle frame had the big baller's nose completely wide open. But trading her body for cash wasn't what had her bank on swole; it was her mastermind techniques that had her wealthy.

When she strutted into the office, she caught Big Dee tossing the night's cash neatly inside a black duffle bag. In her hand, she held a purple pouch that contained the accumulation from the strippers who performed after 2:00 a.m. Coco walked over to Big Dee, with swaying hips.

"Here, baby. It's $2,500 already counted," she said, tossing the pouch on top of the desk that Big Dee had covered with money.

"Thank you, gorgeous!" he retorted as he then turned toward her and looked her up and down seductively.

She was killing the five-inch, blue Jason Wu stilettos and the skin-tight blue minidress.

Damn! This bitch just don't know what she doing to the boy! Big Dee thought, wanting desperately to bend Coco over and fuck the shit out of her. On the other hand, Coco was stalling him out for the first move.

Damn, nigga. Stop looking and . . .

"How soon you gotta be to ya other job, baby?"

'Bout time, nigga, Coco thought, knowing why Big Dee was inquiring about her other job.

"Eight. Why?" Coco retorted with a smile.

Big Dee looked at his Hublot watch and saw that it was only 7:15 a.m.

Plenty of time, he thought.

"Come here, baby girl!" Big Dee told Coco as he then began unfastening his slacks. When they fell to the ground, Coco walked over to Big Dee without hesitating, and dropped to her knees, attacked his erect love tool, and placed him inside her mouth.

"Yes, baby girl!" Big Dee said, running his hand through Coco's natural curls.

"Damn, I love it when you suck this dick with pride," he said.

Neither he nor Coco sensed the danger approaching them, for they were too focused on fulfilling each other's sexual needs. However, perhaps Coco knew more than she was letting on.

* * *

"I see this motherfucka right now, Mauri!" Arab Hajji said into his Bluetooth connected to his ear.

He was on the phone with Maurice while in traffic on his Yamaha 1100 street bike—four cars down from Romel in the second lane. Romel was in a conspicuous pearl-white Impala with a baby-blue top, sitting high on 32-inch Forgiato rims.

"Man . . . let me cap this nigga, Mauri!" Arab Hajji begged Maurice, who was home in bed with Shaquana and badly wanted to be in Arab Hajji's position. Unfortunately, he wasn't.

Damn! Maurice thought, simultaneously sitting up in bed, while Shaquana remained asleep.

"Get that nigga, Hajji!" Maurice said with strong approbation.

"Ten-four!" Arab Hajji responded as he disconnected his Bluetooth and Maurice's call.

Arab Hajji revved up the Yamaha engine twice and then flowed with the traffic as the light turned green. The lane that Romel was in was jammed packed, making it difficult for Hajji to slide over . . . and his lane was no different.

"Damn it! Let me get over, dumbass old man!" he yelled out to the old man driving a luxurious blue Mercedes McLaren.

Uncle-Tom-ass nigga, he thought.

The speed limit on the busy highway was 45 mph, and it seemed that no one was doing 55 mph, which was legal. They were driving east into College Park, no more than five miles from the hood.

I got to get him before he makes it to the hood. Too many cops be in the hood this early, Arab Hajji thought. "I'm going to get this nigga," he said with determination.

* * *

"Ummm . . . uh . . . umm! Shit!" Coco purred as Big Dee penetrated her from the back.

She was bent over the table taking all of Big Dee's enormous-sized dick. Her juices slithered down her legs from her extremely wet pussy as Big Dee dug her back out, with her dress pulled up to her hips.

"Yes, baby! Damn! This dick is good!" Coco yelled out as she felt herself on the edge of an explosive orgasm. She could tell that Big Dee was on his way to exploding too, by the decreasing of his rapid thrusting.

Neither of them heard nor sensed the two Haitians step into the room with Glock .21s in their hands. Their names were D-Zoe and K-Zoe, who were from Miami and working for their new underboss. They both stood five eight and were extremely swarthy. On most occasions, they were mistaken for Jamaican, judging from their lengthy dreadlocks and island features.

"Baby, I'm cumming!" Coco screamed out, climaxing as Big Dee continued to pump in and out of her gushing pussy.

"That's right, baby . . . spit on this . . . !"

Click! Clack!

"Hey!" Big Dee exclaimed, jumping out of Coco and across the table when he heard the irrefutable sound of D-Zoe's Glock being cocked. When he saw the two Haitian men aiming their Glocks at him, he shit himself, causing the atmosphere instantly to reek with the smell of feces.

What the fuck! Big Dee thought as he stared at the two men and Coco, who didn't seem surprised or frightened when company arrived.

"Damn, nigga! You shitting everywhere . . . look!" Coco exclaimed while fanning her nose as the smell of the shit intensified, while pointing at his slacks covered in it.

"Damn, nigga! Why you lose your bowels, huh?" D-Zoe asked Big Dee while pressing buttons on his iPhone.

"He's scared shitless!" K-Zoe joked.

"Damn, Coco! What is this?" Big Dee asked, perplexed.

Coco seems to be with these niggas. This ho setting me up, Big Dee contemplated, until he heard a familiar voice on D-Zoe's iPhone.

"What's up, D-Zoe? How's everything going?"

Tameka, Big Dee thought.

"Boss lady . . . I think we have a shitty problem," D-Zoe retorted.

"It's normal. Coco, I appreciate your loyalty. This shit could have went either way, and you showed me that you were down with the girl . . ."

"No problem. I got you, Meka!" Coco retorted.

"And I got you too, boo. K-Zoe . . . make sure my girl get out of there safely, would you?" Tameka said to him over the phone.

He smiled at Coco, revealing thirty-two 22-karat golds in his mouth, and an elegant smile that made the juices between Coco's legs reinitiate.

"I sure will, boss lady!" K-Zoe retorted.

"Now, Big Dee," Tameka began with a long sigh. "You were good until the end. Much as I disagree, I can't help you out of this one . . ."

"What you mean, Tameka. Who do I need to talk to? I ain't done nothing but—"

"I know, Big Dee. But like I said. If it was up to me, I'd recommend that you stay alive, and I've already spared one life today . . ."

"Who do I have to talk to, Meka?" Big Dee begged.

"Benjamin!" Tameka replied.

"What? Benjamin is dead!" Big Dee said in utter confusion.

"I know!" Tameka said as she hung up the phone.

Both K-Zoe and D-Zoe looked at each other and then at Big Dee. They then aimed their guns at him, and as if telepathically on cue, they both pulled the triggers of their Glock .21s and emptied their clips into Big Dee's body. He was hit more than thirty times in the torso, with the final bullet to his forehead by Coco using K-Zoe's Glock.

"I knew you was a gutta bitch!" K-Zoe said.

"Watch your mouth, nigga! Bitches go in ditches!" she retorted as she handed back K-Zoe's gun and stank walked, swaying her hips from side to side. The trio left the blood-money scene together, leaving the cash on the table.

* * *

Romel had seen the driver on the Yamaha desperately trying to slide over into his lane twice. There was something about his movement that prompted Romel to observe him. He had just gotten off the phone with Markeina, who was on her way to a job interview for an office job, and she wouldn't be back until noon. So Romel decided to come through the hood and let the hood see that he was still alive. With Maurice out, he and his crew would slaughter everything that was affiliated with Romel, but he was prudent and stayed low-key. But he was ready to give it to any nigga—anywhere—that was rocking with Maurice. Romel's senses kicked in when he saw the driver on the Yamaha make a movement by going into his coat and coming out with something that resembled a gun.

"What the fuck is this nigga up to?" Romel exclaimed as he raised up and turned down the Gucci Mane hit blaring from his 15-inch subwoofer speakers. Romel instinctively reached beneath his seat, and then all hell broke loose!

The nigga on the bike found room to maneuver. . . and damn right he had a gun! Romel thought as the man aimed and fired his Mini-14. He took out Romel's driver window and bullet wrecked the entire driver's side, which caused Romel to swerve out of traffic. Romel had no choice for survival's sake but to accelerate through the sidewalk and bushes of a Walmart, which immediately damaged his rims.

"Fuck!" Romel screamed as his bent rims caused sparks. Romel saw the driver coming at him up an aisle, gunning his engine, so he decided to ditch the car or else risk dying in it, because the Yamaha was now putting him against the odds.

Romel had his Glock .17 and hopped out of the '72 Impala, sending a rapid line of fire at the Yamaha 1100. The driver had balls and returned fire, catching Romel twice in his stomach as he slid sideways on the Yamaha between two cars, with a perfectly abrupt stop. Right then and there, Romel knew that he was dealing with a professional—and a maniac.

Clutching his stomach in pain, Romel sent a rapid line of fire toward the direction of the driver and ducked off into Walmart as a bullet from the driver pierced through his shoulder blade. Romel stumbled over customers, knocking them down as they too were all terrified, and scrambled. He had no clue where he was running; all he knew was that it was run or die!

* * *

"Damn it!" Arab Hajji screamed as he watched Romel run off inside the store. He eased the ski mask on his head down over his face and said a protective prayer in Arabic as he rushed into the store with Mini-14 in hand.

I refuse to let this nigga live today! Arab Hajji thought to himself as he entered the store and shoved terrified customers out of his way while searching for Romel.

He's hit! Arab Hajji remembered, so he then looked toward the ground, where he quickly found and then followed the trail of blood.

Romel! Romel! He thought as he hastened his walk, closing in on the trail. He could hear the sounds of cries. Arab knew that he was beyond crossing the line and that he could have left Romel to bleed out. But the intensity of his adrenaline was too great to stop now. He was determined to see Romel take his last breath right there in the store in front of innumerable eyes.

The blood trail turned on aisle nine, and Arab Hajji smiled when he saw Romel slouched on the floor breathing rapidly.

"Romel! Romel!" Hajji said as he closed the distance between him and Romel.

Romel was feeble and in pain, never expecting Arab Hajji to pursue him in the store. His Glock was empty.

Damn! I wish I drove with the AK-47, but who knows what the day promises, Romel thought as

Arab Hajji stood over him. When he looked up at him and the Mini-14 pointed at him, Romel spoke first.

"Nigga, show your face and take me like a real nigga, and not . . . like a coward," Romel said as he winced in pain.

Arab Hajji laughed and then did as Romen requested, by raising his ski mask to reveal his face for a moment, just long enough for Romel to take recognition.

"Fuck you, Hajji! You stupid nigga! You want me that bad to chase me . . ."

"Freeze! FBI! Put down the weapon!" a voice familiar to Romel called out.

It was a woman's voice—sweet and charming. It was a voice that he knew well, but he had to be hallucinating from the pain, thinking that it was who he thought he had heard.

But her voice is unique . . . one of a kind, Romel thought as he heard her voice again.

"Put down the weapon, sir. This is the FBI!"

Hell no! Romel thought as he turned to look in the direction of the female's voice.

What he saw was no illusion. It was real. Agent Clarissa Clemons was wearing an FBI vest and aiming her Glock .45 at Arab Hajji, as were a number of other agents. Arab Hajji looked from Romel, who was now smiling, to Agent Clemons and weighed his options against the sudden odds stacked against him.

Fuck it! he thought as he aimed at Romel's head.

Boom! Boom! Boom! Boom!

Agent Clemons and her gang loaded their bullets into Arab Hajji, only giving him a chance to let off one wild round that missed Romel's head. Arabh Hajji was dead before he hit the ground.

When FBI Agent Clemons ran and knelt down to assist Romel, he looked at her and called her by the name he knew her by.

"Markeina," he said before his world went completely black.

"Suspect down . . . and Romel Jean Baptise is wounded. Get me some medical assistance," Clemons screamed into her earpiece.

Epilogue

Haitian Beny had just finished eating a delicious breakfast cooked by the Latina scullions at his mansion. He had made sure that Big Funk and Corey, who were both working out in the house gym, received a hefty plate of food as well. The fried eggs, steak, cheesy grits, bacon, and ham had this stomach protruding, and he'd made sure to thank God for it.

"Now it's time to smoke me a fat-ass blunt and then . . ."

Before he could finish, his door was taken down by a battering ram, followed by a swarm of FBI agents armed with M-16 rifles. Haitian Beny was partially up the stairs and made a dash toward his room.

"FBI . . . everyone get down. Get him! Take the kitchen. You four to the gym!" FBI Agent Norton commanded his team of agents as he fled after Beny himself.

When Haitian Beny made it to the top of the uniquely designed staircase, he looped around in a sprint to this right, and that's when Agent Norton halted and aimed his Glock .45 at his leg and squeezed the trigger.

Boom! Boom! Boom!

"Awww!" Haitian Beny screamed in pain.

The slugs took him down and ended the chase. It was a victory for Agent Norton.

"Damn, Haitian Beny. I'm afraid that you won't be coming out of this one . . . not even after twelve years," Norton said while placing Beny in handcuffs. He didn't care that Haitian Beny wouldn't be able to walk out on his own. Because he had planned on dragging Haitian Beny out of the mansion like a slain animal.

"Fuck you, Norton!" Beny yelled out in pain.

* * *

It was 10:00 a.m. when Jarvis pulled up to his home. He had bought Champagne an expensive Armani Privé silk crepe gown and some Raye heels that he planned having her wear while making love to her.

Today he planned to make it all about her, if she would promise to wear what he had bought for her—if only for a moment—before she took it off. It was the thought and the contentedness that mattered the most to Jarvis. And he knew beyond a doubt that she would love his gift. He grabbed the Saks bags and emerged from his new Lincoln Navigator, made like it came—luxurious.

When Jarvis entered the house, he at least expected to smell some breakfast. He knew Champagne had skills in the kitchen, especially growing up around Renae.

Maybe she's still asleep, he thought.

"Champagne!" Jarvis screamed as he set down the bags on the sofa and dashed upstairs. He covered the stairs in four long strides. When he got to the top of the steps, he again called out her name. "Champagne . . . girl! Where you at?" he yelled, still getting no answer.

And that's when he sensed something amiss, and he couldn't understand why it felt eerie.

When Jarvis walked into their bedroom, he saw no signs of Champagne. Jarvis realized the house was too damn quiet. When he walked toward the bed, he found a note lying near her phone on the nightstand.

What is this? he thought as he picked up the note and began to read it:

Hello Jarvis . . . we meet again. But I'm afraid we're now opponents! How could you turn so cold on me when you took the world from me? It's okay. We can talk about it. But let's remember the rules no cops!

"What the fuck! Is this some game? Champagne!" Jarvis screamed.

He checked the mansion thoroughly in a rummaging fit before his iPhone rang in his pocket. He immediately dug in his Armani slacks and retried the phone.

"Hello!" he answered breathlessly.

"There you are, champ! Did you think that I wouldn't call you . . ."

"Tameka?" Jarvis said.

"Yeah . . . and guess who else?" she said as he heard a voice in the background.

"Jarvis! Help me . . . !"

"Okay, Jarvis," Tameka said as she waited for Champagne to be taken away so that she could continue her call with Jarvis in private.

"You hurt her, and I will kill you! Do you hear me?"

"Jarvis, I think you're in the wrong position to be giving orders and threats. Now you listen to me . . ."

To be continued . . .

BOOKS BY GOOD2GO AUTHORS

GOOD 2 GO FILMS PRESENTS

**THE HAND I WAS DEALT- FREE WEB SERIES
NOW AVAILABLE ON YOUTUBE!
YOUTUBE.COM/SILKWHITE212**

SEASON TWO NOW AVAILABLE *To order books, please
fill out the order form below:*

To order films please go to *www.good2gofilms.com*

Name:_____

Address:_____

City: _____ State: _____ Zip Code: _____

Phone:_____

Email:_____

Method of Payment: Check   VISA   MASTERCARD

Credit Card#:_____

Name as it appears on card: _____

Signature: _____

Item Name	Price	Qty	Amount
48 Hours to Die – Silk White	$14.99		
A Hustler's Dream - Ernest Morris	$14.99		
A Hustler's Dream 2 - Ernest Morris	$14.99		
Business Is Business – Silk White	$14.99		
Business Is Business 2 – Silk White	$14.99		
Business Is Business 3 – Silk White	$14.99		
Childhood Sweethearts – Jacob Spears	$14.99		
Childhood Sweethearts 2 – Jacob Spears	$14.99		
Childhood Sweethearts 3 - Jacob Spears	$14.99		
Childhood Sweethearts 4 - Jacob Spears	$14.99		
Flipping Numbers – Ernest Morris	$14.99		
Flipping Numbers 2 – Ernest Morris	$14.99		
He Loves Me, He Loves You Not - Mychea	$14.99		
He Loves Me, He Loves You Not 2 - Mychea	$14.99		
He Loves Me, He Loves You Not 3 - Mychea	$14.99		
He Loves Me, He Loves You Not 4 – Mychea	$14.99		
He Loves Me, He Loves You Not 5 – Mychea	$14.99		
Lost and Turned Out – Ernest Morris	$14.99		
Married To Da Streets – Silk White	$14.99		
M.E.R.C. - Make Every Rep Count Health and Fitness	$14.99		
My Besties – Asia Hill	$14.99		
My Besties 2 – Asia Hill	$14.99		
My Besties 3 – Asia Hill	$14.99		
My Besties 4 – Asia Hill	$14.99		
My Boyfriend's Wife - Mychea	$14.99		
My Boyfriend's Wife 2 – Mychea	$14.99		
Naughty Housewives – Ernest Morris	$14.99		
Naughty Housewives 2 – Ernest Morris	$14.99		
Never Be The Same – Silk White	$14.99		

Stranded – Silk White	$14.99		
Slumped – Jason Brent	$14.99		
Tears of a Hustler - Silk White	$14.99		
Tears of a Hustler 2 - Silk White	$14.99		
Tears of a Hustler 3 - Silk White	$14.99		
Tears of a Hustler 4- Silk White	$14.99		
Tears of a Hustler 5 – Silk White	$14.99		
Tears of a Hustler 6 – Silk White	$14.99		
The Panty Ripper - Reality Way	$14.99		
The Panty Ripper 3 – Reality Way	$14.99		
The Teflon Queen – Silk White	$14.99		
The Teflon Queen 2 – Silk White	$14.99		
The Teflon Queen 3 – Silk White	$14.99		
The Teflon Queen 4 – Silk White	$14.99		
The Teflon Queen 5 – Silk White	$14.99		
The Teflon Queen 6 - Silk White	$14.99		
The Vacation – Silk White	$14.99		
Tied To A Boss - J.L. Rose	$14.99		
Tied To A Boss 2 - J.L. Rose	$14.99		
Tied To A Boss 3 - J.L. Rose	$14.99		
Time Is Money - Silk White	$14.99		
Two Mask One Heart – Jacob Spears and Trayvon Jackson	$14.99		
Two Mask One Heart 2 – Jacob Spears and Trayvon Jackson	$14.99		
Two Mask One Heart 3 – Jacob Spears and Trayvon Jackson	$14.99		
Young Goonz – Reality Way	$14.99		
Young Legend – J.L. Rose	$14.99		
Subtotal:			
Tax:			
Shipping (Free) U.S. Media Mail:			
Total:			

Make Checks Payable To:
Good2Go Publishing
7311 W Glass Lane,
Laveen, AZ 85339

CPSIA information can be obtained
at www.ICGtesting.com
Printed in the USA
LVOW04s1432181116
513601LV00008B/406/P